FROM THE AUTHOR

I want to be direct, my name is Greg. I go by "Onision" online. This book is made up of events that occurred in my own life mixed with fiction from the made up life of James.

James is essentially a better version of myself. His home, his school & his life all resemble my own at his age. The people James analyzes and is surrounded by are not so unlike those I've known as well.

I have experienced much of the loss James has however his happier moments are more often than not also mine.

I want to share my story without it being purely non-fiction. I simply felt this approach would make for a far better book.

At points I cried while writing this, at others I laughed. Stones To Abbigale is not just a book I wrote, it is a piece of who I am.

SPECIAL THANKS
Lainey, thank you for editing the first draft.

Erica, thank you for pointing out two word errors.

CHAPTER 1

I was asleep until I met her, when I finally woke I learned the meaning of "perfect imperfection." I've always been the type of person to focus on stars as we spin beneath them, the cool breeze on a sunny day, scattered patches of grass under my feet, the world around me, often forgetting to even glance at the one within. I had remained emotionally unexplored for so much of my life. It's painful knowing some can go an entire lifetime without understanding their own heart, an internal lock waiting for the right key to change everything.

It was the first Monday of November. I opened my eyes, blinded by my recently painted wall-to-wall white room. Even my bed frame, constructed of purely metal, was painted white. It bounced off the walls causing my eyelids to desperately clamp together. Painting my room like this was a clear act of subtle self-inflicted psychological torture. I was going through another phase, from darkness to light, and repeat. Seemed like the story of my life.

My mom could see the darker colors were depressing me, I felt comforted by them, but found there were good aspects of both extremes. I was happy to visit either side, they are both so simple. But right now the intense light bouncing from wall to wall felt like it was ripping my mind in two.

My mom didn't wake me. My alarm clock sat on my dresser with no explanation for its failure to function. The clock only illuminated a blank stare with 8:17 written all over its face. While entirely robotic, I imagined the clock to have the dumbest possible expression, one complementing its failure to behave any way outside its random glitch-infested nature. In the reflection of it's plastic face I could see myself unconsciously making the dumb expression I was imagining the clock to have. I laughed in my casual dorky tone and began to get ready to leave home.

Without breakfast, I left for school with a bogus note in hand to idealistically explain my tardiness. I think most of my teachers were too exhausted to worry about small variances in our appearance from time to time. With how low their pay likely was, I imagined there were very few rules most teachers cared about.

It was another cold day in Lakewood. The wind hit my eyes forcing tears to form in the corners as I sped along the sidewalk at a no-doubt unreasonable speed. I passed Lauren and Raymon walking the opposite direction, no doubt headed toward the nearby church where all the students go to smoke, make out and hide out till school ends. They seemed so childish as they held hands and smiled excitedly as if they had gotten away with some tremendous crime.

Mr. Hanson, my heavy-set, middle-aged history teacher, rolled his eyes as I walked into class. "James, talk to me after class" he said quickly, looking away from me as if I were an undervalued employee who was barely important enough to make eye contact with let alone deliver a full sentence to. "I have a note," I said. He ignored me, and continued his lecture on yet another topic that would not only be completely useless later in life, but wasn't even relevant for even a few seconds after the words left his mouth.

There was only 15 minutes left in the class, but I felt it would be more stimulating to integrate myself into the room to yet again study my classmates' behavior than to sit in a hall watching the rows of scum covered tiles inevitably slide off the decaying walls.

For as long as I remember I've enjoyed seeing how people move around and talk to each other, like they're all animals at the zoo. I would try to deliver a more accurate analogy if I felt there was one but so many of them seemed incredibly unaware of themselves, just living life as if it were some generic predefined routine. Sometimes I felt like an alien who had a VIP pass to submerge myself in primitive human culture just for entertainment.

I sense everything I can take in around me. The seemingly limitless audible tones, tremors in the voices of growing children rang in my ears. In studying people, I found myself gradually learning to literally feel the various personality types I encountered. I hyper analyzed every inconsistent smell, the seemingly random clothing styles, freckles, and assorted hairstyles filled my mind with questions. Trying to rationalize and understand what sequence of events led them to decide who they would become.

I took favor of categorizing most everyone around me. The socially inept know-it-all, the dumb attention-seeking drama kid and the bleach blonde bimbo who gets overly defensive at the slightest hint of criticism. Then there were the kids who just hoped no one noticed them at all. There was so much to be seen, to be considered and organized in my mind.

Class had just ended so I walked over to Mr. Hanson's' desk & placed the tardy note down in passing. As I walked out with the rest of my class, he called after me. "James! We still need to talk!" I responded but continued to walk outside the room. "I have to be early to my next class! Let's talk tomorrow!"

I walked quickly down the hall towards my art class, which was awkwardly placed in a trailer outside my clearly poorly funded high school. On my way to the class a fight had already broken out between two jocks who, no doubt, both had controlling, iron-fisted fathers who brainwashed them into believing conflicts between men are best resolved with the bloodying of their fists. These kinds of men plagued my mind with wonder. I could not conceive a scenario in which they could justify their primitive & pointless mentalities yet they would always continue to perpetuate their self-destructive attitudes as if it offered the slightest legitimate benefit.

Most everyone nearby crowded around the fight. None of them likely cared who was winning, what it was about or how far it went. All they ever seemed to show concern for was their own amusement, always excited to see violence without having to pull out their wallets to pay for it. As the sounds of flesh collided fist to cheek & chest quickly followed the howls from the surrounding students. They would scream "Oooohhhh!" as if it were sincerely delightful to witness creatures like themselves suffer & fall apart before their eyes.

Even if I had time to stop, I never really took pleasure in seeing strangers hurt each other. Most all fights seemed avoidable and were often initiated for a senseless reason. I know, you could say it's more complicated than that, I would like to think it were as well, but reality trumps the way I wish things would be. There's no sense in fighting it when doing so rarely helps anyone.

As I approached my next class the image of Abbi's face illuminated the neon walls of my mind like a projector teasing a theatre screen with fleeting moments of depth & purpose. Ever since I met her, she had occupied a part of my consciousness; whenever I wasn't near her I missed her to an unrealistic extent. You could call my longing sad especially considering we had barely talked; she just had a strange effect on me, one no doubt similar to a willful addiction. There are people in life which we pass by on a daily basis, barely aware of their existence, but on an exceptionally rare occasion you can find a person who fills an area inside your little world you didn't even realize needed filling.

As I walked up the creaking stairs into my art class trailer I could see Abbi was sitting at her shared-desk, alone, same makeup, hairstyle & general appearance I had thought about repeatedly over the last couple days. She was drawing pictures on her blue-lined paper, distracting herself from the cold that filled the oddly glowing room. I smiled slightly trying not to be too obvious and sat down on my chilled metal chair positioned a few seats to the left in front of her. Glancing over, I could see she hadn't moved at all, I felt like she didn't even notice me come in.

I wanted to inspire some acknowledgment of my existence from Abbi so I opened my mouth to greet her when my fingers brushed up against freshly smeared gum under my desk. "Eeew!" I shouted out on impulse. She looked up at me with a blank expression.

Bursting into the room came a group of boys. "Dude I think John's done bro!" one of the other boys laughed, saying "Won't see them for a week at least." I looked back at Abbi to see she also didn't react to their outburst. Strangely knowing that her apathy was generalized and impersonal gave me comfort. Her influence on how I felt was obviously dangerous but I didn't care as no matter how fond I was of the idea that I was not of the world, I knew my place and had no real interest in pretending otherwise.

Jason, one of the boys energetically praising the fight they had just seen, sat in his seat next to Abbi. I smirked watching her shoulders shift away from him. Her body language sent a loud message that she had the same impression of Jason as I did. He was just another moron, placed on this Earth to live his life completely unexamined, a pawn that had no awareness of its own role let alone that it was just another tiny component within a massive unstoppably twisted game. I know it sounds morbid and condescending but my attitude was just something that naturally developed the more I studied human behavior. I would be more optimistic but I find doing so would be like walking into a room with no windows and turning out the light. If you refuse to see the world around you for what it is you're just wasting your eyes.

Art class was about to begin. My teacher, Mrs. Stanley, who looked like she should have retired a ridiculous thirty years ago, approached the front of the room talking about how art is sacred. She also discussed the random object she had us all draw the previous school day and ironically graded it by using her own narrow-minded definition of art. I always wondered how teachers could even attempt objectively grading art. Is there any logic behind validating a form of self-expression using a cold black and white mathematical system?

"Today I'm going to place you with partners" Mrs. Stanley said as she pulled out sheets of paper outlining our activities to come. "To keep this simple, I'm going to partner you with the person you are currently assigned to share a desk with" she said. I sighed knowing I was bound to be paired up with Alex, a guy I had specifically asked to be seated away from ever since he peed in a jar literally right next to me under our desk, acting like he was so cool for publicly exposing himself while simultaneously urinating.

It happened weeks ago and I still can't figure out what kind of crazy it takes for you to, in the presence of people you barely know but have to see nearly on a daily basis, pee in a jar held in your hand just beneath your desk in the middle of a classroom. What then? You show it off like you will be praised and accepted as if it were an accomplishment? Alex, despite being borderline mental, was one of my least favorite people to study. I couldn't help but feel there was some defect in his mind that invalidated the point of conducting a thorough analysis of him. He was completely irrelevant when considering the realities of normal human behavior.

As I was off on a tangent in my own mind I heard a familiar voice ring out, one that inspired the very same emotion you experience when a song you had forgotten you loved, randomly plays in the background of your daily life. "Can I be paired up with James?" her voice was just as I remembered. Despite her having not spoken in class in some time, she hadn't changed a note. Abbi had interrupted the teacher just to partner with me, but I asked myself if was it really just to work with me or just to get away from Jason.

The teacher, looking irritated but understanding Abbi's discomfort with Jason responded "Alex and Jason, you'll be partners. James, switch seats with Jason" "Thank you!" Abbi said with a slight smile. With a cocky grin Jason stood up and in a comedic fashion smelled his armpit. "Wow, I didn't know I smelled that bad" Jason said as he walked over to sit by Alex.

Approaching Abbi was no doubt a way scarier act in my mind than it was to everyone around me, I felt like my head was burning from the inside out. Nevertheless I continued to remind myself that her public outcry to partner with me could have meant nothing. I sat down next to her and did all I could not to turn into a complete dork on her. She reached out and grabbed the project outline that was being passed out. Mrs. Stanley began to read the description of the assignment. "Today you will both be taking something meaningful, but expendable, from your own homes." Mrs. Stanley looked up and emphasized, "That you own!" then looked back down at her paper. "You will tear those items apart here in class. You will then take those items and, using the adhesives, staples and the strings available in class, find a way to create something new out of those possessions." She looked up and said in a low voice sounding somewhat like Dracula "Two, will become one."

Jason raised his hand objecting, "All due respect Mrs. Stanley I'm not breaking something of mine for this class." She replied putting her hands on her hips, "That's fine Jason. We'll supply you with a toilet paper rolls, we have plenty of extras around here." Jason suddenly looked disturbed and sarcastically spouted "Freaking great!" Mrs. Stanley asked, "Are you sure? Your grade shouldn't suffer that much if you two just take Alex's piss jar and tape it to a toilet paper roll. You're already failing this class." Jason couldn't believe what she had just said and Alex maintained an awkward frozen facial expression with his mouth slightly open in his normal weirdo somewhat robotic fashion.

"Oh my god" Abbi whispered under her breath with a slight smirk. I grinned uncontrollably; just seeing her amused was amazing to me. I could hear a scream in the back of my mind reminding me my dorkiness and borderline obsession was escaping through my face. It's not that I couldn't help being in awe of Abbi and basically every little thing she did, I simply didn't want to change how I felt. In a way, she was like your favorite song or book, you could pretend not to like it and in time with the right mental coaching maybe you would sincerely dislike it, but life just felt so much better embracing your condition entirely, letting all your nerdy admiration flow freely.

Mrs. Stanley continued, "If there's anyone else who has an issue, please take it up with my 1800 number which is?" She put her hand up to the air signaling the students to react but only a couple kids replied aloud with her catch phrase. "1-800-BOO-HOOO" they mumbled. She continued, "Good, now for the rest of class please work with your partner on what you plan to bring and draw up a prototype sketch of what you feel your final piece of art will look like." Mrs. Stanley walked to the back of her room and sat down at her 1950's looking rust-infested desk. I would always laugh internally when I looked at the old thing. Maybe it was my way of coping with the fact I attended one of the most run down schools in the state.

"What are you going to bring James?" Abbi asked. It was amazing hearing my name pass her lips but I had no time to think, if I didn't respond right away she would think I was totally awkward. "I... have no idea…" I responded. Smiling she said, "I'm going to bring my hamster cage", I asked, "Did he die or something?" she laughed, "No, I never got one, the cage was just a gift from my dad." "Your dad didn't get you a hamster… for the cage?" I asked. She paused and started to lose her smile. At the first sign of her smile fading I felt a crushing pressure in my chest. "Hopefully you can find something that will work with that," she said. I couldn't help but feel like a total jerk despite not even knowing what I did wrong.

I had the overwhelming urge to fix how she felt so I took a gamble, "Well, I could always bring that weird vibrating thing my mom hides in her drawers all wrapped up in a cloth" I said. She busted out laughing hysterically as a huge grinned filled my face. I was so happy I could get her to smile again. "Eeew! James!" she continued to laugh as the extent of my grin began to stress my cheeks. I couldn't remember a time when I was this obvious about how I felt.

Abbi's laughing trailed off and she paused. Turning to me she said, "You… you didn't actually… your moms?" I responded, "No, I wouldn't know about that, but I'm glad it made you laugh." She responded, returning to a soft laugh "You're more goofy than I thought James." I sat next to her looking at my fingers interlaced in front of me; my wide smile relaxed but still filled my cheeks with warmth.

As class came to a close Abbi patted me on my arm. I turned and she handed me a note. Instinctively I put it in my pocket and said "See ya tomorrow", she just smiled and walked away.

On my way to my next class, I opened the note. I didn't understand why, but it read "NISEONE." Not knowing what to make of it and with little time, I stuffed it back in my pocket to look over later.

Not feeling like skating home, I got on the bus to see all the normal rejects and misfits waiting. Davis, a short and scrawny kid who had been my best friend since middle school despite being one grade behind me excitedly waved me over. "James! Nice to seeeee you!" he said in seemingly the dorkiest way possible. I smiled as he stood up giving me the window seat, knowing very well by then that I preferred it.

As I sat down I began looking out the window, analyzing the little humans running left and right to get on their busses. Something reached out and caught the corner of my eye. I immediately shifted my head to see what it was and quickly realized it was Abbi standing in the parking lot by some beat-up sedan.

"What'cha looking at James?" Davis asked. Without hesitation I began to respond, "Oh, it's Abbi, she's in my art…" my heart sank as I witnessed a boy I barely knew, named Seth, walk up and kiss Abbi on the lips. "James?" Davis said, but by that point his voice was a faint echo in the darkness my mind instantaneously lost itself in. I felt like after a life of numbness I was finally about to truly feel warmth for the first time only to have it all taken away in an instant, leaving me hopeless in the shadows, alone once again.

I looked down at my knees feeling as if I lost all muscle control in my neck. "Are… you ok?" Davis asked. I responded with hesitation "...I'm… just stupid." "No you're not. You're one of the coolest guys I know!" Davis replied. I continued my silence as he offered words of encouragement. "Okie dokie, well, you're awesome and should be super happy so if you want to talk, I'm your buddy so… so I'm here to talk." I was too focused on the conflict raging in my mind to hear anyone at that point. I couldn't think about anything but Seth kissing Abbi the entire trip home.

That night my mom was literally just serving lentil beans she prepared on her crock-pot for the billionth time, a fair exaggeration but still, it was excessive to say the least. My sister was behaving as she usually did at the dinner table, talking about how stupid she thought school was and how she couldn't wait for college. "How was work mom?" I asked trying to keep my mind off the haunting images looping in my mind. "Well, no one at work respects me or listens to me and I generally can't stand it, but you know, we still have food on the table" she said in a stern tone. My sister barked as food flew out of her mouth, "Well at least it's not high school. I'm learning how to be a successful person from a bunch of low-income losers." My mom replied "Whatever your teachers are, they have full-time jobs, which is more than a lot of people can say." My mom gave my sister Lisa a disappointed look. Lisa was well known for showing little respect for hard-working people. To her it didn't matter how much you gave back to society, it only mattered how much money you made.

After the rerun of lentil soup I washed the dishes per my mom's orders and headed to the shower. I sat on the floor of the tub thinking about Abbi, barely feeling the water as it hit my chest. I was so consumed with what I had seen that I had completely forgotten the note until that moment. I quickly reached over to my pants resting on the toilette. I had hoped I read it wrong the first time and that it would make sense with a second look only to see it read exactly what I gathered in my initial passing glance.

"NISEONE" I mumbled to myself. I joked with the idea in my head that she handed me the wrong note but still assumed it wasn't a failed attempt to say "Nice one," which could be taken as a compliment if you were desperate enough. Seconds into looking at the note my eyes widened, having figured out what it meant, I jumped up slipping to my feet and screamed "YEAH!!!" I had cracked it, only to immediately after feel completely stupid for not having figured it out sooner.

My mom screamed through the door from her bedroom "WHAT?" I responded "Sorry! Nothing!" I hurried to finish showering.

Staring at my phone wearing only a towel, I smiled as I typed in "NISEONE" or "647-3663" into the number keys. I assumed we shared the same area code otherwise she likely would have given me a longer sequence of letters and I was right. After two rings I got an answer.

"What do you want?" a disgruntled man's voice asked. Like a bad engine struggling to start in a monster movie I clumsily belted out a response "I... uh... I was looking for..." An unenthusiastic female voice in the background said, "Give me the phone." "Whatever" he said dropping phone in front of her. "Hello?" I could recognize the voice now it was Abbi. Trying to hide my excitement by maintaining a normal tone I said, "This is James." Abbi excitedly screamed and responded "Oh my god you figured it out!" Hearing her optimistic tone I laughed saying, "So… why…" She interrupted. "I was hoping to find out if you figured out what you're bringing to art class." I said "Oh!" and looked quickly around my room. I couldn't see anything immediately so I just said, "I'll… surprise you!" She then replied "Oh come on, tell me." My eyes locked on to a plausible item for the project. "How about my… bear… I'll bring my bear!" I said. She replied "Oh, ok, oh! I have an idea. Instead of the cage, I'll bring in a stuffed animal of mine and we'll make like, a zombie bear." I laughed "Awesome" I said. "Ok, I'll see you tomorrow ok?" she replied happily. I answered "Ok, byeee." Just before she hung up I could still hear her laughing, leaving me with a sense of accomplishment and a lasting smile as if it were painted across my face.

CHAPTER 2

The following morning Mr. Hanson approached me in the hall before class started. "We're supposed to talk," he said in his usual stern voice. I responded, "I know, but what about?" He began gesturing with his hands as he often did, I guess it was a habit he developed to trick people into believing he was saying something interesting. "You know you're a smart kid, but you keep showing up late to my classes and it's becoming a problem" he said. Surprised he showed genuine interest; I replied with a smirk, "I'll do better in the future." He continued "Alright, well, I also wanted to ask you about a TA opportunity." I replied, "You don't have a teacher's assistant?" I watched a bead of sweat fall down his balding forehead as he responded. "The last TA moved, and yeah, you're not always on time, but you get your work done honestly and efficiently." I asked, "Ok Mr. Hanson, next semester?" He authoritatively replied "No, you can just take an elective class credit and I'll let your current teacher know you'll be working with me from here on."

I immediately thought of the possibility of losing art class and rejected the idea. "My only elective is art class right now and I don't want to give that up" I said. He took a step back looking offended and lost his temper, in a disgruntled tone he said "Art? Art class is a joke James! Tell me one person you know who is making a living painting pictures!" All the students nearby in the hall stopped and looked towards the shouting. I looked at Mr. Hanson unaffected, reminding him I would not give it up. I wasn't about to sacrifice the one class I had with Abbi for alone time with a sweaty, anger-prone history teacher.

Mr. Hanson looked at everyone stopped in the hall and screamed "Oh ha ha, everyone look at Mr. Hanson he's such a goof, move along kids!" Everyone just looked at him as he turned back to me, maintaining his clearly frustrated posture. He then waddled into his classroom to begin class. I reluctantly entered with the remaining students to sit at my desk, which was conveniently placed within broomstick range from Mr. Hanson's desk.

After enduring another useless history lesson revolving around my home state of Washington it was finally time for art class. I walked as fast as I could without looking too awkward, in my normal fashion, only to find Abbi wasn't even in the room. I sat down in my new seat and waited, only to see everyone but her fill the room.

Mrs. Stanley closed the door to our class trailer and instructed us to begin dismembering the possessions we brought from home. I began cutting the bear with a scalpel Mrs. Stanley provided me but my muscles seemed to work on their own as I found myself consumed with Abbi again, her overwhelming presence on the edge of every thought fragment in my mind. Just a short while into class I found myself looking down at my bear, now cut into 6 pieces. I felt like I was in a science lab dissecting an actual animal, the most noticeable difference being that the cotton stuffing didn't look like or stink of old flesh and death like real animals did.

Later that day during lunch, due to my mom not being able to afford buying me a cell phone, I used a payphone to call Abbi but got no answer. I didn't feel like eating so the rest of lunch I just sat on a bench outside staring at people interacting with each other.

I made a major effort to distract myself knowing that focusing on what could be was mostly a waste considering I was so powerless to influence any change at that point. Even just watching the bushes move around in the wind made more sense to me than letting worry consume me.

Later that night after I had just finished my shower I placed the one cordless phone we had in my house next to my bed on my windowsill. I would have dialed her but I didn't want to call more than once a day for fear of wearing out my welcome.

That night, a few different calls came in but they were always for my sister Lisa. Her receiving a barrage of phone calls from random guys was nothing new to anyone in the house.

The normal conversation you could expect to hear Lisa take part in, with excessive projection in her voice, would most always revolve around how stupid she thought other girls at school were and how she hates basically everything about Lakewood High. I didn't want to know what she was talking about, ever, but my TV volume couldn't compete with her voice. It was like she thought she was so important, everyone around her just had to hear everything she had to say no matter how trivial the topic.

After a couple hours she finally stopped running her mouth so I turned off my TV and with it my room faded to darkness. I welcomed the silence like a warm blanket on a cold night.

I woke up the next morning to see the phone sitting there just like my stupid alarm clock, useless and unbearably annoying to look at. I expected it to sound off at some point but like the clock it failed to deliver.

It was raining outside; clouds filled the sky in normal Lakewood fashion. I wasn't going to skate to school this time out of fear it would rust my skates and hinder my ability to skate fast if even at all. Instead I decided to ride the bus, pretending for only moments I really had a choice. As I climbed up the bus steps, Davis rang out "Hallelujah, James is here to save everyone from the evil clouds!" I genuinely smiled for the first time that morning thanks to him. As usual I sat next to the window seat that Davis courteously always offered me.

The beginning of history class was the same old story. As usual I barely paid attention. I just thought about Abbi and hoped she was ok. Interrupting my thoughts of Abbi came a very rude outburst by Jason. It was odd to hear his voice, as I wasn't supposed to see him till art class. He stood outside our closed class door waving his hands in hopes of disrupting us. It was clearly for no real reason more meaningful than a toddler would have in invoking chaos around their immediate environment. Some people just want to get an emotional reaction to their behavior so they can feel a sense of power or control.

Jason began banging on the door so Mr. Hanson walked over and opened the door and asked "Why aren't you in your class?" Jason responded saying, "Got kicked out, what's up?" "Go stand outside your class till it's over" Mr. Hanson commanded, Jason rebelliously replied, "Don't tell me what to do fatty." I could see Mr. Hanson was about to lose it, so I interrupted. "No one wants you here Jason." Mr. Hanson looked back at me with a look of surprise. He seemed shock I would say anything on his behalf. Jason became extremely silent, now refusing to look anywhere but at me. His glare was intense but it seemed so forced, like he wasn't really offended but didn't want to look weak in front of everyone else.

Mr. Hanson then closed the door inches away from Jason's nose but that didn't stop him from staring intensely through the vertical window slot in the door. He remained so still and consistent in his stare, it was almost as if he had become a red-faced almost cartoonish portrait hanging on the door.

As class came closer to an end Jason was no longer staring at me and wasn't even visible from my perspective. Knowing Jason had something left to prove, many of the students naturally assumed he was somewhere within the immediate vicinity. I could tell most everyone was concerned as they kept looking back at me, wondering what I was going to do about the clearly unstable and enraged jock that no doubt was still lurking just outside our door. Every kid in there knew I couldn't just hide out in the class. I was sure this was some kind of victory for Mr. Hanson. He knew I wouldn't have this immediate problem had I accepted his offer to TA for him. My decisions led me to this; I built a doorway to certain destruction and I knew if I was going to be brave, I had to walk through it.

I didn't have time to deal with hesitating once class was over, seeing Abbi was my real priority. I walked out with the class just like I normally did only this time Jason was following close behind, as I'm sure most everyone assumed he would. I was about to leave the main building to head over to the art trailer only to feel a hand grab my shoulder. The hand slipped as I pulled away, nails scraping along my skin to clamp on my shirt. I was then yanked swiftly back from the main hall door. It began.

I yanked my shirt aggressively out of his hand and clutched my now scratched up shoulder. I was now facing Jason who immediately lunged at me and threw me into the already half-broken hall door just behind me. I bounced back from the impact and pushed Jason in the center of his chest to distance him from me so I could continue walking away. Without hesitation he used my response to justify further violence and began throwing punches. I was knocked to the ground within seconds and he began trying to pull off my backpack resulting in me being briefly dragged across the floor like a helpless child. I was now a couple yards away from the door I was trying to leave through. I twisted away to return to a standing position while simultaneously snatching my backpack back so hard that it flew out my hands and smacked the door behind me, leaving a huge crack in the glass. I could hear glass falling off the door behind me.

People began to gather around us, and like a chemical reaction they began screaming just as they did before. Much of what was happening was a blur, but I remember they would scream every time Jason hit me throughout the irrefutably one-way fight. It quickly got to the point where I didn't even feel the punches, I could only hear them laughing and yelling as Jason swung again and again. I kept falling over and over but every time I would return to stand only to fail at defending myself from further blows. I didn't block a single hit; I didn't even throw one punch at him.

As my nose began to bleed one of the boys my sister was friends with, Matthew, grabbed me and pulled me out of the fight. He was twice my size but was also on Jason's football team so naturally he did nothing to help me win. The only thing he offered me was an end to the beating I was suffering.

Shortly after the fight ended I found myself sitting on a mattress in the nurses' office, not allowed to leave, not allowed to do anything but think about what happened. Despite everything in my head feeling scrambled and disorganized, there was Abbi, waiting in the same place, just as she sat in the back of class. She radiated warmly in the back of my mind.

As lunch approached Principal Leeman came into the room I was staying in at the nurses' office and asked me how I was feeling. I responded "Well, my tooth is chipped, my chin hurts, my face is bruised and I just got humiliated in front of my peers." Mr. Leeman said, "I've gotten multiple statements saying you pushed him. What's your response?" I replied "I pushed him back after he pushed me first. All I did was push him back once and then he did this to my face." I made a circular motion around my face showing how one-sided the fight way. Principal Leeman said in a commanding voice "Well he's suspended for 10 days," he paused and I felt relief assuming the Principal was on my side, but then he continued, "You will be suspended for 2 days." I was surprised they would suspend someone for just pushing back when they are pushed. What was I supposed to do? Just ignore being assaulted? If school is meant to teach us how to survive in the real world, and in the real world you are legally allowed to defend yourself, how could they justify this punishment?

Principal Leeman informed me I could finish up the day and not return for the following two days. "You should be at least grateful for that, Jason was escorted off school grounds entirely," he said. Principal Leeman stared at me sitting there, helpless and about to break down. "Ok then, see you again in a few days" he said and quickly walked out. All I could focus on feeling in that moment was the tacky ice pack on my face and a sinking feeling of worthlessness. It's not something I like to admit but the truth is I cried seconds after Principal Leeman left the room. The type of cry you suppress but your eyes still get become red, your body trembles & painfully hot tears still fall. It was the type of sadness that made a person ache to their core but you do your best to hold on, to not lose yourself to your emotions like you would so carelessly do as a child.

I sat in the room alone till I could collect myself. Shortly after I gathered my stuff and proceeded to finishing my classes for the day. I also asked a couple of my teachers about any work I would miss so I could keep up while I was suspended but didn't have the motivation to stop by every single class before leaving the school entirely.

As I was about to get on the bus home I looked over to see Abbi again in the parking lot with her boyfriend Seth. They were standing by his car. This time they were not showing affection, in fact she seemed like she wasn't even willing to look at him despite him clearly and aggressively speaking to her.

Without a second's thought I shifted away from the bus and began walking over to Abbi to see if she was ok. The more I could hear Seth's tone as I approached the more worried I became.

Seth reacted to me like a guard dog in a ghetto-fenced yard once he realized I was headed towards him. He puffed out his shoulders and glared at me in attempts to look intimidating. Abbi remained upset, it seemed like she was emotionally unable to look anywhere but the ground.

Now within a fair speaking range, I tried to sound optimistic for the sake of Abbi's emotional state, "Hey Abbi, were you at art class today?" I asked. Her boyfriend stepped in front of her to block my view and said, "Are you the kid that called her the other night?" I responded, "Yeah, we're…" "Just ignore him James" Abbi said mumbled loudly behind Seth.

Seth looked back as if an arrow had just been plunged into his chest. Abbi then walked around him looking only at me and said, "Will you walk me…" but paused when she saw my face. Abbi's facial expression changed quickly to shock as she asked in an alarmed tone "…what happened?" Her boyfriend busted out laughing, "Oh, you didn't see this idiot get wrecked by Jason? He didn't even fight back. I would've had that jock prick choking in his own blood in seconds but you just took a beating like a…" Abbi interrupted screaming, "Shut up Seth! You sadistic freak!" Seth's grin turned into a scowl. He rapidly stepped towards her so I blocked his path by stepping in front of him. Seth looked more mortified than I had ever seen a person get. In such a short time knowing him I could see he had a number of mental and emotional issues, more so than I understood.

Seth didn't even try to get past me to Abbi; he let his voice reach her with his screams "You have no respect! After what I've done for you?" Abbi replied, "I'm sick of this Seth, I want nothing to do with you."

Her voice cracked as Seth screamed once more. "If you're ending this again! I..." He didn't know what to say, but in his eyes I could see a deep intense hatred. When I looked in most people's eyes I saw all kinds of things but in him there was only anger and pain. His hands were shaking furiously, his breathing noticeably irregular, he was losing it.

Abbi still refused to look at Seth as he threw his tantrum. He yelled "Fine! Be with a guy who can't even protect himself! Idiot!" Seth got into his car as Abbi tightly grabbed my arm; her eyes remained closed like she was scared, hiding in a shell. She jumped at the sound of Seth slamming his car door.

Recklessly, Seth floored the gas pedal and his car lurched forward, barely missing Abbi and me as he pulled out of the parking lot. Abbi stood silently by with her eyes still closed. I didn't know how to act in a situation like this. Trying not to make things worse I just said, "I will walk you home, to answer your question." Abbi opened her eyes but remained silent. She nodded.

We had been walking for a while, every step making us feel like we were slightly further from our problems. She finally spoke, "So I was in Art Class and I saw your cut up bear." I responded, "Yeah? Creepy right? Maybe it was a FUBAR idea." She laughed a little. "Yeah, I guess we're both kind of weird, I was all game for it." I softly laughed as I began to feel raindrops hitting my arms and neck.

"I hear running is just as bad as walking in the rain" I said "You get just as wet?" she replied "Yeah, something like that. It's like the harder you try to fix some problems, the worse they get." I impulsively asked to confirm what I had earlier seen "So your... Seth... is..." She interrupted "Hopefully soon completely out of my life." My curiosity overtook me, I asked, "What happened?" She frowned and said, "Other than what happened in the parking lot?" I responded "Well, I mean, I donno, don't say anything you don't want to."

She stared at her feet as we continued to walk. I noticed her makeup was running. Shortly after she noticed too and began to rush us getting home. Walking faster she said, "I'm sorry, I really don't want you to see me like this." She continued to rush slightly ahead of me, I stopped walking and said "Hey!" she slowed down and stopped still facing away from me.

We stood in the rain for only a few seconds before she asked, "Do you think makeup really helps anyone?" I replied still looking at her back, "I think it helps us forget what we don't want to remember, it let's us pretend we're a little more perfect than we really are." She laughed sadly and said, "That's one way to put it." I smiled and replied "Makeup is just makeup, and skin is just skin. It is what it is."

Abbi looked up at the rain for a moment and then down at the ground again. She then turned around with her rain-soaked face revealing what she was hiding under her makeup. Standing before her in the rain, looking at the results of what she had suffered, it broke my heart. Abbi wasn't worried about her makeup running for the reason I thought, she was just afraid of what I would think when I saw the bruises on her face, some just like mine.

"Do you see them?" she asked with a quiver in her voice. Without restraint I responded with the first thing that came to my mind, "I see beautiful girl, who I very much enjoy walking with in the rain." Despite her face being covered in falling drops of water, I could clearly see tears fall from her eyes. Her head fell forward as she began to shake, her tears falling almost in sync with the rain. I walked up to her and put my arm around her side and walked with her the rest of the way home.

As we got to her doorstep I said "I'm just seven letters away, call if you need anything ok?" she smiled and nodded. "See you tomorrow?" she asked. I replied, "I got suspended for two days". She looked offended "Woooow! Punishing the guy who got beat up, classy!" I responded, "Yeah… well, I pushed him back." She replied "Clearly not hard enough." I laughed sadly looking down as she unexpectedly wrapped her arms around me.

Despite it being so cold out and her being soaked, it was the warmest hug I had ever received. I hugged her back, said goodbye and walked home with a huge smile on my face, bruises and all.

CHAPTER 3

Briefly after I fell asleep that night I had a dream about Abbi, it was the first dream I had experienced in some time.

I'm not normally the type of person to be deeply impacted by dreams as more often than not I can control them. I can recognize the fact that I'm in a dream and twist things around so that whatever is making me afraid becomes afraid of me. This tactic however could not possibly work in this soon-to-be nightmare, as there was no living monster waiting around the corner. There was no emotion in this machine that was about to reveal itself to me. I could only watch without a physical form. I was just a helpless spectator in my own mind.

The dream began without any sound; only a deep hum accompanying what appeared to be Abbi laughing in a field of what looked like gray grass from a far. As my view of her revealed more detail I began to realize that what I thought was grass was actually long slender claws. Experiencing a more alarmed spectrum of emotion, the audible hum cut out and was replaced by Abbi's screams. The sounds echoed bouncing off the walls of my mind splitting me in two and engulfing the core my being.

She was not forming any words in her screams and I began to understand why the more I analyzed every detail. I shifted my perspective to a new angle. I was now above her looking down and could see the claws were pulling her into the ground. She showed no resistance to being dragged into the ground, she didn't even cry for help, she would only scream in pain as she slowly sank beneath the surface. I began to distinctly hear blades and gears violently turning just beneath her.

It's difficult to explain, but in her eyes I could see she didn't want to be saved as she genuinely felt she had earned the suffering she was enduring. She believed she deserved to be ground up until there was nothing left.

Once she was pulled completely under I was finally given a physical form in the dream. Dropping from above I landed on the soil she disappeared in. I immediately dropped to my knees and began digging with my bare hands to get to Abbi. I was only inches deep before the ground ripped open forcing me to jump back.

A deep canyon began to form central to where I had begun digging. The splitting and groaning quickly gained momentum. Ripping and screeching sounds erupted all around me as the earth divided before me at a now crippling rate. A hellish sight consumed my eyes as I looked down on the collapsing landmass below. Powerful machines wielding massive blades swung violently scraping dirt and rock with a sound so tremendous I could only faintly hear the screams of countless desperate humans below.

I quickly realized the terrified voices beyond the ripping blades were no illusion. Thousands of lives were being devoured in piles, no person among them begging for life rather, like Abbi, they screamed only from pain delivered not just by the roaring blades and gears, but their very existence itself. Suffering & consciousness had become one in the same.

I then woke up to my room filled with sunlight, but it could not change the darkness my dream left me with. I felt something inside me change, almost as if I had seen something I was never meant to and now had to find a way to lose the thick cloud freshly looming over my head.

It is as I said briefly before, I feel like a visitor here, like I'm in this world but not a part of it like everyone else. I study people and situations to find out how they work and sometimes my dreams fill in the emotions and thoughts I missed while I was awake.

Not having to go to school that day due to my suspension I decided to write a letter to Abbi. It read:

"When I look in your eyes... I at times feel a level of sadness I have never felt, as if we, despite barely knowing each other, have been apart for far too long.

When I talk to you it is like I am listening to a voice I've ached for yet haven't heard in a lifetime. Every other experience I have with you seems familiar but at the same time, it hurts, like you would feel if you begged for something and only received it when you had already given up hope.

These feelings are all so strange and evolving at a rate that scares me as they are for someone I am only just now truly getting to know.

Even with my brief presence in your life I've picked up on so much suffering and almost feel powerless to create any change. There are so many wounds, so many scars, so much I only know enough about to fear. I'm trying to understand.

Abbi, you have more pain in your life than I can imagine. I hear it in your voice, I see it in your eyes and in the way you move. I just want to see you smile without there being an ocean wall of tears behind your eyes.

I want to hear everything you have to say. I want to find a way to heal the damage done until you can forget it ever existed."

I sent the letter to her email address, moments later the phone rang. Answering the phone I heard Abbi's voice on the other end. "Hey, can you meet me at the Quick Shop?" she asked. I responded, "Did you see my email?" she replied "Nope, why didn't you just call?" I said, "It would've been really hard to say over the phone, I had to find the words." She replied, "Ok, I'll look and then I'll head over." I then confirmed "Sure, see you there".

Shortly after, I got dressed and skated over to meet her. I arrived quickly, thanks to what seemed to be a record speed for me. However once I arrived I found myself waiting for someone who now had no intention of meeting me. I could only assume I had just made myself look like a huge jerk to her. I attempted to call her from the nearby payphone and she didn't answer.

As I skated home, in my mind, I went through the letter I wrote over and over. I began to blame myself, concluding based on her absence that I must have dug too deep too fast. I scared her away because I reacted on the emotions I experienced in that dream before actually considering the human being on the other side of the letter.

I felt like I was just about finally connect with someone only to ruin everything at the last minute.

CHAPTER 4

My suspension had been lifted and I had just arrived back at Lakewood High. Approaching my history class I could hear people snickering as they watched me walk by. Someone screamed "Wuss! Learn how to fight!" behind me but I just kept walking.

As I sat down in class Mr. Hanson walked up to me, he placed his hand on my shoulder and spoke under his breath so others would not hear "Don't worry about the work you missed, ok James?" I looked up at him and he gave me a slight smile. I suppose it's because he felt bad that I was beaten up shortly after trying to get Jason to leave the class alone. It was a lucky break too considering Mr. Hanson's class was one of the few I didn't stop by to see what work I would miss before beginning my suspension.

I approached the art trailer feeling panicked over what to expect. I hated that I said anything to Abbi, that I overstepped my bounds and acted like I knew her when I was only going off my own dream-influenced emotional intuition. I felt a conflicted hatred towards myself for jeopardizing a relationship with someone that was so important to me. If she did give up on me, I could only blame myself.

Opening the door I could see Abbi wasn't inside, instead there were just pieces of my bear sewn to pieces of her bear sitting on her desk. Maybe I was reading too far into what it meant, I could really only hope that there was something left to us that I could sew back together.

Walking closer I could see something sticking out just beneath the bear. It was a note that read: "James, meet me behind the church when you get this." Immediately, I thought of the church neighboring Lakewood High.

I stuffed my backpack inside the desk and quickly made my way off campus to meet Abbi. As I approached the church there was a strong forceful wind blowing behind me that made it feel as if I was being pushed to her by nature itself. I felt like a fool for thinking that, I'm far too unimportant for any significant force to consciously influence my life. I walked around the church only to hear Abbi say loudly "James!" I turned to see her standing under an overhang that reached out from the church.

I walked over to her and began to apologize for the letter, but she cut me off saying "Why did you write that to me?" I responded "I wanted to separate myself from everyone else in your eyes. I wanted you to know I was trying to understand you, all of…" She interrupted "How messed up do you think I am James? How screwed do you think my life is exactly? Because if you had any social skills, you might know that saying to someone what you did, is… I'm not damaged goods… I'm not broken!" Her voice was giving out as she began tearing up. "I'm sorry... I was..." I said, helplessly watching tears fall down her face.

"I was wrong... but I'm here, and I will be as long as you let me." I said. She wiped her tears and struggled to speak. "The reason you saw what you did, in my eyes, my voice..." she continued to struggle as she cried "You saw the bruises from my ex, but you wanted to know everything." She paused to wipe her tears again. I listened carefully as she continued to speak "James... I haven't been beaten just one or two times..." Abbi said as she looked at me as if every word was agonizing for her to say. With tear soaked eyes she continued, "I've been violated beyond that James... by people who called me their friend, people I trusted took advantage of me and that killed so much of who I am... who I was." her face was consumed with stress, her body shook but she managed to continue, "My mother abandoned me and left me with my father who doesn't even care if I live..." before she could finish I wrapped my arms around her. She dug her fingers into my back as she pulled me closer and cried into my chest.

As we held each other I said, "You were never damaged, only changed. Any part of you that you think died is just hidden, waiting to come out when it's safe..." Abbi squeezed me even tighter. I continued, "Every time I see you, you become more beautiful to me than before." She gripped me more tightly than anyone ever had. She was finally hearing everything she wanted someone to say to her and I was saying everything I wanted Abbi to hear, that is, most everything.

CHAPTER 5

I sat alone in my room thinking about all that happened in the last day. As I slid deeper into thought a knock sounded at my door. "Dinner's ready James" my mom said. I responded "Lentils again?" She opened the door and looked at me with a blank facial expression "We have to talk, come to the table."

As I left my room, I saw a man sitting at the table next to my sister. Trying not to be rude I said hello and he smiled responding loudly "Hello! Nice to meet you James!" I asked my mom "So who is this gentleman?" My mom responded, "Go ahead and sit down James." I slid out the old-fashioned second-hand store chair I always sat in at the table and waited for my mom to explain.

"This is Rick, the reason you haven't seen much of him is because he lives on the other side of the mountains all the way in Spokane," my mom said. I smiled feeling slightly awkward and replied, "Oh, alright, cool." My sister immediately mocked me "Oh, cool mom duh! You're such a dweeb James." Despite her bratty insult, I could see she too felt awkward about Rick being so spontaneously introduced to us and was just trying to distract.

"Rick and I have been dating for quite a few months now and are starting to become quite serious" my mom said, clearly seeking our approval. Rick added

"So yeah, it's really cool to finally meet you, your mom talks a lot about you". I smiled and nodded while thinking about how odd it was my mom had never mentioned him.

Rick proceeded to tell us stories about him hunting animals, his upper-level position at a construction company based out of Spokane and continued to remind us how happy he was to be meeting us. As far as I could see he wasn't a bad guy but as usual, I didn't expect much knowing most everyone puts on their friendliest mask for first impressions. I'm sure my sister was thinking pretty much the same thing I was, he wasn't my mom's first post-dad boyfriend.

My mom inquired, "So how's your life going James?" I replied "Fine." Rick asked, "Got a girlfriend?" I didn't respond. I just kept my head down, looking at my plate. My mom looked at me with a proud smile, "James is more of the mysterious type Rick, he doesn't talk about his relationships." Rick then said "Oh yeah? Well if you find a lady half as good as your mom, I'd say you're set." My sister interrupted "Aren't you seeing that messed up emo chick James?" Looking over at my sister with a blank face I said, "Aren't you seeing every guy at school Lisa?" Lisa looked horrified and my mom responded "James!" not knowing what else to say. Rick was the only one still smiling at the table at that point.

Moderately upset by what Lisa said I asked to be excused and went to bed.

As I climbed on the bus the next day Davis hollered "Praise be to James! Our hero has arrived" I smiled as I always did. I hated loving his hilarious lines; they were kind of a tradition for Davis. Every time I stepped on the bus, he would yell them. Even when I wanted to be upset he always found a way past the walls I had built, knowing exactly what to say every time.

As I sat next to him he said, "I've been missing your face a lot Mr. James, I'm trying to figure out ways to compete with your skates." I smiled and said "You're one of the only reasons I ride the bus Davis, you're doing just fine." Davis then jumped up and yelled, "You hear that everyone, my best buddy thinks I'm pretty fantastic!" I laughed, wishing to myself I had more friends like him.

As I approached my history class, I could see Mr. Hanson waiting in the hall. I tried to walk by him unnoticed but he said, "Not so fast, you need to go see the guidance counselor." I asked why and he replied, "It's about that fight you got in. Ms. Robertson is waiting." I proceeded to the office where there was a line of three people ahead of me. It wasn't due to bad scheduling, Ms. Robertson was just outmatched by the school population and considering she was the only person most students knew to get free condoms and/or advice from she was regularly seeing visitors.

"James Patrick!" she said aggressively as I approached the old wood and glass door. I smiled out of politeness as she turned to the others and tossed a bundle of condoms in their direction. "These are a last resort, abstinence first!" she said as she stood by the door waiting for me to enter. One of the boys standing at the door said "I actually need advi…" but she slammed the door before he could finish speaking.

"Have a seat James," she said. I sat down and the room filled with a few awkward seconds of silence. She continued, "So it looks to me that you're healing up ok." I replied confirming I was fine. She then said "I've heard both sides of the story and have concluded that your friend Jason is destined for not so great things if he keeps up his attitude." My face remained still, emotionless really. I just sat silently listening. She asked, "What direction do you want to go with your future?" I replied, "I've heard really great things about up." It was like my joke hit a brick wall. She seemed only sarcastically amused and continued speaking, "But seriously, I was told you turned down a TA position which I personally recommended to Mr. Hanson." I replied, "I just wanted to stay in art class." She replied "With Mrs. Stanley?" I nodded and she laughed. "So who's the girl?" she asked. I was surprised that she concluded so quickly it was even about a girl. But then again I was just one of thousands of students, we like to think romance is unique, but we're most all playing the same game. Ms. Robertson had years dealing with people like me, no wonder she could see right through me.

For a brief moment, Ms. Robertson nearly spoke my mind, she said with a smirk, "Oh come on, lots of us like to think we're special but that just of shows you how we really aren't. Especially the brats walking these halls." Knowing Ms. Robertson had to keep our conversations private, I replied, "There's this girl… Abbi. I really like her, and it's the only class I have with her." Ms. Robertson was no longer smirking now that I told her who I was interested in. She sat up and looked down at her desk. She moved some items around and stopped suddenly, she then looked me in the eyes and said "Listen to me carefully, I can't tell you anything about Abbi but I can give you advice, think twice about getting involved with her. I want to see you succeed and some people being a significant part of your life can make that difficult for you." I didn't say anything, in that moment I was lost in thought wondering why she would become so serious over Abbi.

Ms. Robertson then asked, "So, I'm not going to try and change your heart, in my experience that's more often than not a lost cause, but I can change your schedule to something that fits. Abbi has PE during third period, how about you just stick with Mr. Hanson after your first class of the day. Doing so will replace your art class, and your third period will now be PE, where you can see your precious Abbi." While her attitude towards Abbi continued to concern me, I also was curious as to why both Ms. Robertson and Mr. Hanson were so adamant about having me be a TA, but I was grateful they were at least trying to work with me regarding my preferences, so I accepted the schedule change.

I returned to Mr. Hanson's class and requested I attend art class one last time before the schedule change. Mr. Hanson agreed and I made my way over to the art trailer once more. As I walked in the trailer door I was happy to see Abbi once again sitting in the same seat she always did.

When I approached her to sit down she pulled out my backpack and shook it, "You're backpack has a lot of interesting things in it." I replied "Oh really, you went through it?" She responded "Yep! And by interesting things I mean nothing, just school junk." I laughed and asked "Life's got enough burdens for us to carry, why add physical weight?" She raised her eyebrows and said "Ok smarty, did you like our bear?" I smiled and replied, "I love it!" She threw her arms up and hugged me. Mrs. Stanley walked in, immediately seeing our hug and said, "If you're going to suck or eat go find an alleyway. This is a trailer we have god damn dignity!" Not knowing how to react, I looked over at Abbi silently mouthing "Oh my god" to me. I smiled and sat down with Abbi.

Alex walked in the room and gave me a glare, probably because his art partner was still suspended for the fight we had, which meant he had to do it alone. I tried to ignore Alex, all I could think of is that pee jar when I looked at him which still freaked me out.

As class came to a close we gathered our things and began to walk out. "Bye Mrs. Stanley I'll miss you." Mrs. Stanley responded calling me the F word, in her natural offensive fashion and gave the class an awkward, semi-shocked laugh.

Walking outside, Abbi asked, "Why do you think Mrs. Stanley still has a job?" I replied "Pretty sure everyone feels they'll guarantee themselves an eternity of torment in the afterlife if they were to fire someone as old as her." Abbi replied "Yeah, I guess it would be hard getting a job when you're resume lists World War I nurse in your work history." I laughed so hard I had to stop till I could control it, "Are you ok?" Abbi asked with a nervous smile on her face. Still laughing, I said "Sorry, sorry." and continued walking as Abbi looked at me, bewildered by how funny I thought she was. My reaction wasn't really just about what she said, but the fact that she said it to me. I felt so important and excited when she gave me her attention.

As we got closer to the gym Abbi was giving me a funny look, as I normally didn't walk her that far, I said, "Don't worry, I'm not stalking you, we have the same class now." She replied, "Manipulating your schedule to be with someone sounds like stalking Mr. Patrick." I said, "Not if you drop Mrs. Stanley." She pushed me playfully saying "Jealous!"

The boys split off to dress in their locker room and the girls did the same. I didn't have gym clothes with me yet so I just sat down at the bleachers and waited for everyone else to get done putting on their uniforms.

A deep voice sounded off "What are you doing here kid?" I looked over to see a very tall man in the baggiest gym suit I'd ever seen. "Hi, I'm James Patrick, I think I have your class now. You can clear it with Ms. Robertson. "He smiled and said, "Well James Patrick, I'm your gym teacher Mr. Mack." I nodded and smiled as he bluntly asked, "You're that kid who got beat up by Jason?" I replied, "Yeah I pushed him after he pushed me and then he started throwing punches." He smiled and said "Well, that's my nephew for you." I froze up and blankly stared at Mr. Mack as his words sank in. I swear I could feel my heart skip when I acknowledged his connection to

Jason. Seeing the look on my face Mr. Mack continued "Don't worry, between you and me, kid's a prick. Just like his dad." Mr. Mack chuckled and walked away. I felt relief and awkwardly smiled only to see Abbi in the corner of my eye bursting out of the girls' locker room. She was in her PT uniform and carried a beautiful smile on her face.

Running over to me, Abbi sat down and gave me a big hug. "I'm so glad you're still in a class with me," she said. The gym shirt was hiked up her arms so I could feel her skin connect with my neck. The sensation was glorious. My face was beaming from feeling her warmth around me. I replied, "You will be the one reason I look forward to gym." Mr. Mack overheard and interrupted as he stood a short distance away "Hey kid, and I thought we were becoming friends!" I laughed awkwardly feeling a little weird about him eavesdropping. But then again, it's much easier to close your eyes than it is to turn off your ears.

Everyone gathered on the gym floor, excluding me. Mr. Mack immediately noticed I was not participating and said "Hey, if you don't have gear, go in my office and pick out an outfit." I reluctantly got up and walked over to his office where all I realized I would have to sift through a huge pile of mismatching jerseys and sweatpants to get a half-decent outfit.

After changing in the bathroom I walked out to everyone taking part in dodge ball. I could feel the focus of the room shift on my outfit and, just as I expected, I was greeted with laughter.

"Hey, at least you won't get your normal clothes sweaty from dodge ball!" Mr. Mack said tossing me a ball as the game was already in play. Before I could even catch it, Raymon, one of the jocks in the class, smacked me in the side of the head. Everyone but a few people bust out laughing again as Mr. Mack lurched up and pointed at Raymon screaming "You're out Raymon, can't hit above the shoulders!" Raymon replied with a discouraged snap of his fingers, scowling as he sat on the sidelines. It was odd how he broke the rules and hit another person in the head yet pretended to be the victim. I never really understood the human tendency to feel sorry for yourself when you're being punished for breaking rules you were well aware of.

Abbi was on my team and we were down to just a few people, I very quickly found out I was quite good at the game, better than I thought at least. I kind of used Abbi as my motivation to do well. I imagine it was some kind of evolutionary thing, a man trying to impress his mate with physical performances to demonstrate his superiority over other members of the tribe.

I kept catching every other ball thrown at me only to return it, hitting a student approximately one out of every three attempts. I always threw low to decrease the chance of anyone catching my ball. After a while my consistent efforts paid off, our entire team was back in play. Raymon had made his way back in the game on their side but only a small nerdy kid remained in play with him. Raymon would try to catch what we threw but was always a few inches short of reaching the ball as it flew by. A ball smacked the nerdy kid in his ankles and only Raymon was left. He tried to throw a ball at my head again but this time I was ready. Just as the ball flew past me every person with a ball on my side threw theirs at him. In an almost comedic fashion every other ball impacted his chest and below. We were all cracking up over it but Mr. Mack interrupted us letting us know class was over.

Before Abbi ran back to the locker room, she walked up to me and said "Can you call me tonight?" I nodded smiling and she kissed me on the cheek. My mind exploded with excitement. From that single kiss on my cheek my whole body felt light and warm the rest of the day.

After doing my chores later that night I called Abbi like she asked and she answered "Hey you!" I replied "Not a lot of callers huh?" She said "Actually I just embarrassed myself on the last call hoping it was you.

My grandma felt pretty special for about ten seconds".

She and I talked for hours; we discussed the plausible absurdity of horoscopes, "The Secret," the legitimacy of souls, the afterlife and even leprechauns. Very few topics were off-limits. Being free to talk about whatever was on my mind felt liberating. Having these conversations with her served as just another reminder that there was someone out there who could really understand me with just as much kindness and acceptance as I did them.

Before I hung up I said "Abbi, thank you for making my imperfect life feel perfect." She laughed at how cheesy the line was only to respond, "Well thank you for being so perfectly imperfect." I felt a warm smile come across my face and said goodnight.

CHAPTER 6

Quite a few days passed. Everything felt like it was falling into place with Abbi. She had become the center of my world and I felt like I was finally really finally enjoying my life.

One morning my nose woke me up, there was an unfamiliar but pleasant smell filling my bedroom. For the first time in a long while breakfast was ready for my sister and me. My mom had made eggs and waffles. To my surprise Rick was, again, sitting at our table. Him being there completely explained why my mom was making breakfast.

I approached everyone already sitting and said good morning. Rick seemed a little nervous and again my mom asked that we all have a talk. I sat down not so sure of what to expect. Rick spoke "Listen, I don't want to tiptoe around this topic. Your mother and I want to move in together." My sister's arm went limp as she was attempting to eat making her fork smack against her plate as she dropped her jaw simultaneously. While she was normally overdramatic about most everything, her reaction pretty much summed up how I too was feeling this time. My mom tried to soften the blow by saying "And yes, this is going to be a pretty big transition for all of us but we'll make it through."

It began to hit me harder as I thought things through; there was no way Rick was moving in with us, our little condo was already overcrowded. Rick was the one with the higher-paying job, which meant most everything I knew was at risk to change. I began to feel panicked, "You... Mom I have Abbi." I said. My mom looked concerned and Rick blurted out "Listen, we're not going to break up your relationship for the sake of ours, we'll figure something out ok?" I felt like I was going to pass out; I kept thinking about the horrible timing, that I finally I had someone I bonded with more than anyone else and they were going to make it far more difficult for me to be with them, because of what? Rick had said it would work out but I barely knew him. I had learned some time before to trust people on what you know them to be, not what you hope them to be. Rick hadn't been around long enough for me to see him in a significantly positive or negative light and in that, I realized hope was all I had.

I stood up and said, "I'm sorry, I'm not hungry. I'm going to go wait for the bus." Everyone silently sat at the table awkwardly pushing around their food as I gathered my things. As I was brushing my teeth I could hear my sister crying and ranting dramatically in the background. Once again, she reacted externally how I felt inside.

Davis could see my upset posture out his window as the bus pulled up so as I walked up the steps this time he screamed, "I love you so much! I wish you were my boyfriend!" I hated myself for giving in yet again, but laughter escaped me. My life was turning completely upside down and Davis was there to make me experience a fragment of happiness.

As I sat down, Davis grabbed me and hugged me. Someone sitting a few seats ahead screamed "Eeew homos!" which made Davis yell back, "I love him! This is love!" He jumped onto the seat with his little body and pressed our faces side-by-side "Look at our love!" I patted his arm that had been wrapped around me sarcastically and he released me to sit down. Immediately he asked "So what's up buddy? How can I turn that frown upside poopy poo poop?" He could see I was still a bit upset and didn't really want to talk so he did his classic "Well, I'm always here!" It was nice having Davis to keep me afloat

Since I began my Teacher's Assistant work with Mr. Hanson I felt buried in needless information about his job. He was constantly ranting about the low pay, working conditions and hours. Despite all this he would still remind me about how happy it made him to see some students overcome the horrible condition of our school and succeed regardless.

Ms. Robertson would stop in from time to time while I graded papers. Whenever she visited she and Mr.

Hanson would bombard me with questions. They would ask me how I liked being a TA, random questions about the state of the school and discuss academic politics. I kind of felt sorry for Ms. Robertson, we never had normal conversations, it was almost always about her job, almost as if that was all she knew.

While she was visiting that day, Ms. Robertson could tell I was upset about something so she asked and I confessed I was pretty bummed out. I wasn't specific because I wanted Abbi to be the first person to know what was going on between my Mom and Rick. Ms. Robertson replied "Well, this better have nothing to do with you know who." I found the fact she was still butting into my relationship with Abbi to be incredibly annoying. I said nothing in response hoping ignoring her bringing up Abbi would give Ms. Robertson the hint I didn't want her talking about Abbi.

Finally it was time for PE and Abbi greeted me as happily as she ever did. I didn't want to ruin her day so I asked her to call me later that night to talk without hinting too much regarding what it was. Despite my efforts she could see it in my eyes, she said "If you have something on your mind, I really want you to tell me." I tried to think of the best way to say it but couldn't, so I just told her that I had to tell her later. She replied "After school?" and I agreed.

Throughout gym class her behavior changed completely. She picked up so well on my concerns that it consumed how she interacted with almost every person and thing around her. The mere worry of some bad news caused her to appear significantly depressed, almost as bad as before we began talking.

Abbi was waiting by my bus as I walked out of school. I had been thinking about the best way I could tell her all day. "You have to tell me," she said before I even finished walking. I didn't delay my response as she had waited long enough, "My mom's boyfriend is talking about having my mom move in with him, he said he'd make things work with you and me despite the change." Abbi kept looking back and forth at me, then to the side, speechless. I continued, "I can't leave you behind." She interrupted as tears already began forming in her eyes "I can go with you." I paused in disbelief; in a single moment she expressed as much desperation for me as I had been feeling the last few days. It was as if every action she took repeatedly proved her perfect alignment with my intentions. We were becoming like gears turning in sync, unable to be slowed or broken by any obstructions. She waited for a response, looking at me nervously. I smiled and said, "Actually, I was thinking I might be able to stay here alone. My mom owns the condo and I'm 17, so I donno."

Abbi's nervous expression faded slightly and she said "Have you talked to your mom about that?" I replied with "No, but I won't let us get split up, and…" I paused still in disbelief that she was willing to come with me if I left. Abbi started to smile, feeling more certain I wouldn't leave her behind. I continued, "I'm glad you… said what you did. I know now either way it should work out." She giggled excitedly and immediately jumped on me while simultaneously wrapping her legs around me happily kissing every part of my face but my lips. I said "Whoa" laughing and thinking in the back of my mind about how surprisingly easy she was to carry.

Later that night, I spoke to my mom about potentially staying home and continuing to go to the same school considering I was graduating the next full school year. She seemed hopeful but said she had to talk to Rick who had returned to his home past the mountains to work.

When we spoke on the phone Abbi and I mostly stayed away from talking about the move. We focused on topics like colonizing the moon, strange creatures we have yet to discover in the ocean and if robots will become so much like humans one day that they'll begin to have the same legal rights as us. Some topics were pretty silly but we didn't really care, it was just fun to hear what we could come up with talking about things we barely imagined till then.

At some point in the night Abbi brought up a more serious topic. "I noticed something about you, when we're in gym class." she said, I replied asking her to elaborate, she said "It wasn't just in class, once I saw it I began noticing it everywhere. You barely pay attention to any other girls, even when they talk to you. You rarely even look at them most the time." I laughed and replied "I do that intentionally you know?" she asked why and I continued "Because I don't want to risk you thinking for a second you're not the most important person to me." she replied in an amused tone "Even when I'm not around?" I added, "When you're not around, I like to pretend you still are. So in a way, there's no such thing as being without you." She warmly laughed and we quickly went back to much lighter topics.

Abbi wound up falling asleep on the phone with me. Listening to her rest, how peaceful she sounded. Despite knowing it wasn't true, I couldn't help but feel like everything was still perfect.

CHAPTER 7

I found myself fallen, somewhere deep in a conscious state of unconsciousness, some place I can't remember. It may sound strange, even ridiculous, but I felt like I opened my eyes while I was asleep, and saw only black. Not as if I were blind, but as if the rest of existence had simply disappeared and I was just, alone. It wasn't long before I woke to find myself submerged in reality once more. Thoughts of Abbi quickly greeted me as I adjusted to the experience of my physical surroundings. For a week now I had been constantly reminding myself how lucky I was to have a relationship that actually made sense. Abbi never did anything that I felt betrayed me or exceeded the bounds of reason.

Davis was sitting next to me on the bus, he was talking about his Lego collection and how he loved matching colors in a sequence within the structures he assembled. He said it made him feel like there was some balance and order to his life in a weird way. While I listened to Davis my thoughts partially remained on Abbi. She continued to fill my mind with hope no matter where I was or what I was doing.

We arrived at school on, you guessed it, another cloudy day. I know it was unreasonable to assume, but I often felt like our school was the darkest place in the city. It was as if every morning the clouds would execute a biased agenda against our school all for the sake of depressing every poor soul who attended it. The wind was blowing. Looking back, I felt like everything about that morning was screaming at me to wake up and see what was really going on. But I couldn't see it; I don't know how I could have. Dramatic events have a way of sneaking up on us, leaving us only with feelings of remorse and thoughts of what could have been.

Davis got off the bus behind me tripping a little. A normal kid would have gotten upset, but Davis, as usual, found a way to turn it into something positive, he even laughed as he stumbled. I turned to check on Davis to make sure he was ok when I heard a loud popping sound ring off towards the school. My immediate assumption was that a car in the back parking lot had just backfired. There were a lot of crappy second-hand cars at our school so it wasn't unreasonable, but still, I assumed wrong. Davis and I heard screams immediately after, in a way the wind seemed to turn the screams what sounded like a chorus, one familiar to the haunting dream I had about Abbi now many days past.

Hearing more popping sounds and screams in the wind I instinctually I grabbed Davis' jacket pushing him back towards the bus. Students who weren't aware of what was going on due to the heavy wind and competing noise from the bus engines reacted as if we were being inconsiderate jerks. To shake everyone into reality I screamed, "There's a shooting! Get back on the bus!" A sudden panic took over everyone within the vicinity.

The bus driver who was already looking around, suspicious of the faint sounds he heard, reacted as well, "Get on the goddamn bus!" he screamed. I could hear some students begin to cry out of panic as we all rushed to duck down behind the bus seats. The bus driver slammed the door shut leaving behind a few students who had already walked too far away from the bus. The driver, despite being a grown man, was freaking out like everyone else and, as a result, found himself crashing our bus into the one parked immediately ahead of him. As the bus's collided our bodies smacked into the seats ahead of us. One student wasn't even hiding behind the seats yet and flew forward to land face down in the aisle.

The bus driver, quickly recovering from his mistake, backed up to maneuver out of the drop off area. The window by my seat fell off the side of the bus and shattered on the ground while the front windows also began to detach after being impacted by the earlier collision. A thunderous gust of wind burst through the void left by the fallen windows. With the wind came the sounds of even louder gunshots and screaming as if the shooter was closer to the front of the school. I was too scared to look but someone else had locked their eyes on the front door of the school and screamed "Seth!" A sense of absolute horror overtook my body and tears began to flow from my eyes.

If Seth was really shooting up the school I knew that meant he would be looking for Abbi. All fear left my body. Thinking only of only her I leapt up and screamed, "You have to let me off right now!" The bus driver ignored me initially; he was too concerned with getting away from the school. He probably didn't even hear me with everything that was going on. The inconsistent and forceful acceleration forced me to fall back in my seat, countless thoughts pounded through my head and yet every other word screamed Abbi's name.

My mind was numb; the wind surged through my hair. Everyone around acted almost like magnets, helplessly nailed to the dirty floor. I was the only one sitting in a seat, completely lost in thought. My eyes staring off a thousand yards, my skin pulsating with heat, I felt like I was a bomb only minutes away from detonation. I remained silent, still, waiting for my numbers to fall in sync. Waiting for my mind to green light an act that would change my life forever.

I had a moment of abnormally intense clarity. Seth had irreversibly lost his mind, I could only suspect he would likely blame his broken state on Abbi after their last encounter. I couldn't take thinking about it for more than a few seconds. I sprinted up to the driver and screamed, "If you don't let me off, I'll jump off!" The bus driver plunged the bus into the side of the road violently, as a result I stumbled falling hands first onto the bus dashboard. The driver yelled, "You got a death wish, that's your choice but I'm getting everyone else to safety!" He opened the door and aggressively motioned for me to get off. By the first wave of his backhand I had already bolted out. I violently ripped my backpack open and tried to put on my skates while maintaining my speed towards the school.

After only a few seconds I was skating at full speed. I could already hear the first of many sirens to come far off in the distance as the gunshots continued to ring in the heavy air. My whole body felt like it was jumping out of my skin. Tears continued to pour from my face from both the wind hitting my eyes and the war raging in my mind.

As I approached the school, I could see freshly fallen bodies by the door exactly where Seth had walked out as our bus left. I could've sworn they were all still moving but my eyes were blurred from tears and I knew many if not all of the shots were fatal. I didn't know much of anything about human anatomy, but through the blur I could tell Seth was shooting people mostly in the neck and head, leaving little for medics to work with.

I fell to my knees at the entrance whipping my legs around while simultaneously straining to take off my skates. The floor was too slippery with blood to move anywhere on those tiny wheels. My pants already had bloodstains from the bodies near by. I had no time to focus on what was happening, I had no time to consider anything but Abbi's safety. I ran off in my socks, one barely even on my foot, leaving everything at the entrance, I felt I was running entirely on an autopilot function I didn't even know I had.

In only seconds I saw more blood than I had seen, let alone imagined, in my entire life. The inside of the school was soaked with the sounds of sobbing students who weren't shot but too scared to move or even function. One student, clearly in shock was just crawling down the hall wailing and shaking. The thought of Abbi shook me out of the sorrow I felt for that student. The first place I could think to look for Abbi was her locker and I was already half way there. I approached and found nothing, no one was even shot in the area of her locker, and I had to look elsewhere.

As I returned to the entrance area of the school I crouched next to a table and froze in place to listen for any sign of where Seth was; it felt like minutes, but I imagine it was only seconds. My state of mind likely altered my perception of time, every survival based operation functioning to its maximum ability aside from my flight instinct that demanded I run and hide like the rest. Another gunshot had finally violently shattered the sound of whimpers and lungs desperately choking for air as they filled with blood. The gunshot sound was distant as if it went off outside, on the other end of school.

Sprinting off in the direction of what I had already accepted as potentially my final destination, Abbi remained at the forefront of my mind.

Bursting out the side doors of Lakewood High I crouched and froze in place again. My senses once more ignited. I immediately heard a voice scream out "I will not let you do this you psychopath!" It was an old woman, the only old woman I ever knew to go anywhere near the trailer classrooms just ahead. It had to be Mrs. Stanley.

I shot forward like a cannonball being fired on a long awaited enemy. Even the wind felt like it had stepped aside to let me pass without resistance. As the art trailer came into view I could see Mrs. Stanley approaching Seth, she stood tall without any indication of fear. Seth was dressed in a long white coat with a pure white outfit underneath. This was all clearly premeditated; like he wanted to proclaim how much blood he had shed, not just around him, but on his body as well. He got what he wanted; he was drenched from collar to shoe in the blood of his fellow students.

Despite Mrs. Stanley's aggressive stance, Seth barely paid attention to her and limped by her trailer as if she didn't even exist. I assumed his crippled posture was the result of the unfathomable reality he had found himself faced with. What he was subjecting everyone to, the mortifying level of terror and suffering was like nothing he had likely imagined. Going back wasn't an option on any level; Seth was already dead to the world for what he had done. He had to have known there was no peace in life left for him in life. No place to hide or chance of ever feeling safe from judgment or persecution again.

Mrs. Stanley screamed at him again, "You are an embarrassment! A disgrace! How dare you, you scum!" Upon hearing her verbal condemnation without hesitation Seth whipped his gun toward her like a sword being unsheathed, time again felt like it had drastically slowed as his weakened arm struggled to steady his aim. I ran at Seth as he screamed in pain just from the weight of lifting his gun towards her. Mrs. Stanley tried to step to the side of the shaking muzzle but maintained her advance on him clearly hoping to disarm him.

I was just about to reach Seth to attempt disarming him when out of nowhere his gun flew in the air and Seth yelped as the air left his lungs. I screeched to a halt in my blood soaked socks trying to process what was happening.

My watery eyes and adrenaline was clouding my perception, possibly even more now than before, but I was able to process that another student had tackled Seth. I almost immediately identified the student as Jason from his size and clothing type alone. The very same boy who had chipped my tooth and pummeled my face was now beating Seth senseless.

In such a strange way I could sense within myself a glimmer of deep satisfaction, not only from the realization that Jason had single-handedly cut the head off this otherwise ongoing tragedy in our lives, but instead that he had without a doubt clearly held back when he was fighting me. This time I could see Jason was letting out every ounce of brutal rage he had within him and unleashed it all on a desperately defeated Seth.

Mrs. Stanley turned her back on Seth, still being dominated by Jason's fists, leaving him for dead to go help other students. I collapsed to my knees, gasping for air as I heard Seth's face being repeatedly impacted by the fists and elbows of a justifiably enraged Jason. "How could you do that to my family? To all of us! Do you think you accomplished anything you bastard? You sick freak!" Jason screamed at the now unconscious bloodied face of Seth while showing no intention of letting up.

As I calmed my breathing, not forgetting my priority for even a moment, I quickly began running through Abbi's daily routine at school. Her class just before art was Human Anatomy, which wasn't far from where I was. Running back inside the school I leapt over fallen chairs and abandoned possessions only to find Abbi's class completely empty. She was nowhere to be seen. I immediately reminded myself she was normally early, which made me begin to feel she had escaped safely as there was only one door out, a door that to my knowledge had no bodies near it.

I ran taking the path of least resistance out the front entrance to see students gathering near the school property line. They were bundled in a tight-knit group behind the trees immediately outside the bus drop off zone.

Despite my aching feet and intense stress I reached the group in little time, now missing a sock and my feet littered with broken glass gathered throughout my search for Abbi.

Most all of the girls were crying while many of the boys were giving a thousand yard stare, their eyes locked on the school.

Pushing myself through the group I could see Abbi sitting on the ground in the upright fetal position. An overwhelming sense of relief consumed me as I fell forward to wrap myself around her.

She was shaking and whimpering uncontrollably. I immediately said, "I'm so sorry I wasn't there." She lurched up only then realizing I had found her. She grabbed me with a strength beyond any embrace we had had before, I never imagined she was so strong. Abbi was unable to say anything over her crying, as a wave of emotion continued to overtake me I had nothing I could say either, we remained speechless together.

Through the group of students' legs I could barely see the lights from police cars pulling up to our school. Everything seemed like it happened over a period of 40 minutes but it was in fact a small fraction of that. Soon after I witnessed unmarked cars, ambulances, and SWAT had all responded with a similar level of urgency as well.

We could only sit and wait as the police sorted out everything that had happened over the next few hours. After some time I was able to report on what I saw as I sat on a curb while a medic pulled glass out of my feet. They were all out of ambulances and stretchers so I was grateful just to have someone to help me get patched up since the adrenaline was no longer distracting me from the pain.

We were given blankets as we waited outside, Abbi refused to be more than a foot away from me for a single moment. We were both so incredibly relieved to still have each other, as if we were vital parts of the same system, one not being able to maintain their stability without the ensured safety of the other.

Off in the distance, I could see a large amount of empty body bags being delivered. The entire area was swarmed with every emergency response service you could imagine. Not far behind stood a group of reporters, significantly expanding in size every passing hour.

Not too long after my feet were bandaged and I had given the police all the information they asked for, I was able to leave with Abbi. As we headed towards the cordon I saw my mom waving her arms just outside the police-establish barrier. Upon seeing her, the immediate sad reality sank in both our minds that Abbi's dad didn't even bother to show.

Knowing what I was thinking Abbi tried to reassure me and likely herself in the process. She began saying her father probably didn't even know there was an emergency but pointed out that he was probably still recovering from being drunk the night before.

As I walked into my mom's arms she became the second woman that day to show me a strength I never imagined they had. Her hug, while painful, offered me an unforgettable sense of comfort. As she embraced me she revealed to my surprise that she had already been briefed on how close I was to everything that went down.

Continuing to hold me in one of the longest hugs I had ever experienced, she told me how mad at me she was while also expressing how simultaneously proud she was of me for running into danger when so many people ran away.

I imagined she assumed it was to help everyone in the school but the truth is, I could only feel selfish knowing I wasn't doing anything for anyone but Abbi. I was ashamed and somewhat terrified by how little I seemed to care about most everyone else outside her.

The love and compassion being expressed towards me continued to leave me speechless. I felt Abbi rubbing my back as my mom continued to lock her arms around me. Abbi's physical act of affection triggered a thought causing me to jolt upright. I quickly asked my mom if Abbi could stay with us that night and she responded positively. Her one stipulation was that we had to stop by her Dad's house to first get his consent.

We all got in my mom's car and drove to Abbi's house. My mom approached the entrance of their home by herself knowing we were basically unable to do anything outside repeatedly revisiting what had happened earlier that day. She knocked on the door multiple times and got no answer. She then walked back to the car and said "Hey Abbi seems no one is home want me to get your things for you?" Abbi replied, "No it's ok I'll get them myself, my Dad's kind of crazy about intruders, wouldn't want anyone..." Abbi stopped speaking and simplified things "Be right back."

My mom opened the car door for Abbi and she hopped out to quickly raid her room for the essentials. Before I knew it she was outside again with a bag full of her things. She was so quick to pack that it occurred to me leaving her place on the fly might've been more familiar to her than I knew. Remembering her brief comments earlier, I imagined there were many times where her home had become such an emotionally hostile environment that she was rendered unable to stay causing her to seek most any way out, even if it meant she was leaving one sinking ship just to climb aboard another.

My mom began talking about how happy she was that my sister had skipped school that day. She said, "Who would have thought her rebellious attitude and disregard for her future might have saved her life?" Had we not been through everything that day, we would have given at least a slight laugh but found ourselves all sitting in an awkward silence.

After cleaning ourselves up, Abbi and I walked into my room leaving the door open as a comfort to my mom. This was short lived, the end specifically occurring after my mom had walked into her room and closed the door. Our door closed with hers.

Initially I had offered Abbi the bed implying I would take the floor, but she sat down on the mattress and expressed almost exactly what I was feeling "After everything we went through today you lying next to me is the only way I'll feel any comfort tonight" she said softly. I was relieved and laid behind her through that night and a few nights to follow. She called her dad at home repeatedly in the days after to let him know what had happened, but he still didn't answer.

As was expected school had been canceled for a couple weeks. This reality left us to consume our time with the news, talking about the people we recognized in the photos they showed and checking in on various people we talked to at school over the phone, including Davis who had no problem getting upset at me for the first time in a long while for abandoning him on the bus as I did. Fortunately in natural Davis fashion, his frustration was quickly followed by jokes and words of encouragement.

Abbi and I didn't know how to feel about so much of what happened. Through our time away from school we shared many moments of sadness, reflecting on the faces we would never see again, hearing the sad speeches of those left behind by the fallen, but most of all, our expressions of sorrow erupted from our own experiences. The images and screams still echoed in our minds.

Aside from sadness I felt an almost equally intense sensation of numbness. After a short time I found the only comfort that consistently broke through my shaken state was the warmth of Abbi pressed against me night after night. She was my sanctuary.

CHAPTER 8

Lakewood High struggled at first, we all did, but as promised the school was operating once again and welcoming students back. Abbi had returned home a few days prior, telling me how much crap she was going to give her dad for up and abandoning her for so long. But we both knew he rarely showed any interest in what she had to say. I suppose we both liked to think of our father's in a way that made us feel like they could care, from time to time.

In a strange way we both felt safer after the incident, knowing someone who had beaten Abbi, someone who had terrorized her life, was now completely unable to harm her again, or anyone for that matter. We learned he had barely survived Jason's beatings but was left in a coma according to the news reports in both the papers and on TV.

On our first day back reporters from all over the country and even a few countries outside the US gathered around the school to witness our recovery process. Shootings had become so common in the country but ours was regarded as particularly significant due to the fact Seth had claimed a staggering 52 lives, leaving only 4 of the people he shot still alive. All those lives, connected directly to countless family members, friends, all now subjected to a heightened risk for depression and, statistically, even suicide. Seth had directly taken so many, but the collateral damage done was beyond what any of us could likely imagine.

Signs on all the new school doors instructed us to gather in the gymnasium. I headed to Abbi's class to catch her so we could sit together. She was smiling and gave me a warm hug from behind. She said "You're always there for me, I have no idea what I'd do without you here." I replied "You don't have to worry about that Abbi, at this point you're basically a core section of my programming." She smiled "There you go again with your robot talk." I smiled as I walked down the hall with my arm around her.

As we entered the gymnasium, the only noise I could hear was the sound of shuffling bags and the banging of shoes against the bleachers. Barely anyone was talking and most everyone just looked concerned outside a couple small groups who were only quiet out of respect for the situation. Many of the students had not arrived at school yet or were evacuated before they could see anything. The amount of psychological damage avoided by that reality alone gave me a sense of comfort. Just knowing people with gruesome images in their head that they absorbed first hand were in the minority felt like small victory.

Abbi and I sat next to Davis who looked more upset than I had ever seen him. He looked up at me and somehow found a way to still mumble off "Hey buddy, nice to you see you." I smiled and looked on waiting for the administration to begin speaking.

A man in a long black coat and suit walked out and introduced himself. "Hello, I am Donald Richof, I have been assigned by the President of the United States to address incidents like the one your school has bravely endured." We remained silent as he continued "I'm not going to fill this room with empty idealistic words, even if I tried, many of you would identify them for what they were, complete and utter political nonsense utilized poorly as a means to save face." he paused and cleared his throat.

"Our president believes in transparency and remaining relevant to reality, not deluding events to appear as some act of any unexplainable influence. This was a school shooting, one like many of the shootings you have heard about and while it may appear in many pessimistic minds that your government is doing nothing to make changes so this will not happen again to another group on such a significant scale, I want you all to stop for a moment and think of your cell phones, clocks, televisions, computers etc. What you see on the outside is rarely the full story. What you see is only the surface, the illusion created to make us believe simplicity surrounds us, but underneath this thin shell, this illusion, dwells a massive and complex system that is working to achieve a goal. Every single event brings us emotionally and mentally closer to absolute intolerance. We will not rest till drastic measures are taken to help prevent tragedies like this from occurring.

While many of you have already reached the point of complete intolerance, having seen this heinous crime unfold first hand, much of the rest of the country fails to empathize; they have not lost friends, they have not lost teachers or had their entire lives thrown into chaos. They are fortunate to have the luxury of ignorance as an option, but their luck can become a burden to the rest of us. Their oblivious state can only hurt those like many of you, who are living the reality we have no choice but to accept."

"In closing, the President has decided to speak to each and every individual class later this week. It is not a photo opportunity. There will be no press in the rooms. The President of the United States has made a personal decision to single handedly handle your questions and concerns, to help in whatever way he can."

There were many sounds of shock indistinguishably surrounding the gymnasium. Many of us never imagined we would ever be able to see the President in person, let alone be able to talk to him.

Mr. Richof continued, "I would now like to direct you to the screens on each wall to your left and right where you will be hearing from someone many of you know and care for." The lights darkened as the projectors shining a school logo on the walls went blank. Distortion now illuminated the screens as if the inputs were being shifted.

The screen immediately after revealed my gym teacher, Mr. Mack, sitting back in his partially tilted upright hospital bed with a bandage over his face, and another covering the side of his chest. Gasps rang out all over the gymnasium, many covering their eyes to momentarily escape, leaving their mind seconds to process and accept the state of one of the school's most beloved instructors. Mr. Mack had refused to speak to reporters since the incident and most everyone was just glad to see he had, at the very least, survived.

He began to speak. "Students of Lakewood High, you can see me, but in this room, I'm just talking to a camera. I'll do my best to get through what's been running through my mind the last few days that I've been conscious." He paused looking down, beyond the side of his bed. He was, no doubt, imagining the fear that a lot of us felt. Mr. Mack wasn't like a lot of teachers who divided themselves emotionally from those he educated. He most often treated us as if he was one of us and, while we loved him for it, we all still respected him enough to recognize his authority.

Resuming eye contact with the lens Mr. Mack continued. "As you can imagine, under my bandages are gunshot wounds. The bullet that was, no doubt, intended for the center of my forehead, instead shattered bones in the side of my face. The bullet that wounded my side was meant to hit my heart, I consider myself fortunate. The reason, obviously, that I am in this state is because I directly encountered the gunman and in my case, attempted to disarm him. Despite the initial gunshot to the side of my face, I was able to hasten my approach towards the gunman. I was shot in the shoulder instead of my heart, due to the irregular movements I made in attempts to take his weapon away. As a result I was able to snatch the M16 this young man was armed with & I used the butt of the rifle to impact his windpipe. When I smacked his windpipe, I quickly recoiled and repeatedly hit his arm as he went for his secondary weapon. I'm not sure how much damage I did, but I did my best."

The students stared in awe, completely taken in by his story, as he continued, "Seth, the gunman, began scrambling away from and before I could fire to disable his ability to further harm anyone, I, unfortunately and regrettably, lost consciousness." Mr. Mack's facial expression shifted, making his disappointment in himself evident. Mr. Mack struggled heavily in attempts to speak further. We all sat silently and respectfully as he found the words. "I was told that the only people who were shot after crossing me were survivors. The 4 students who were only wounded, I was informed, likely lived because of his inability to properly aim the only remaining weapon he was armed with. His disability was a result of the damage I had inflicted on his neck & and arm with his own weapon." He became silent as the information engulfed the room.

In only seconds the entire room roared to life with bone-shaking cheers. We had realized many of us owed our lives to Mr. Mack, that without him, Seth would have been able to continue using his automatic rifle, the very same rifle that claimed the many lives lost that day. There was no telling where we would be without Mr. Mack's bravery and self-sacrifice.

After moments of cheering, Mr. Mack continued "As you may have heard on the news, the gunman had planted explosives around the premises that he had planned to detonate once he ran out of ammunition. The explosives would have had an effect similar to what you would expect of napalm and, no doubt, would have destroyed most everything within the school itself. Over the last couple weeks, authorities have repeatedly scanned the premises with K-9 units and detection equipment to ensure the school offers an even safer environment than it did before."

"I hope you will all continue to be strong through this hard time, and I need you all to…" Mr. Mack paused looking off to the side again. He continued, "I wanted every single one of you to know, I'm very sorry for all of your irreplaceable losses. I also want to thank Jason. He, as you are all very well aware, was able to bring this event to an end. He is certainly one of the bravest amongst us." Mr. Mack finished speaking and the projectors returned to the school logo.

The principal of the school approached the center of the stadium and ensured us school would continue as normal. He went through a speech on what the nation had learned about shootings and how we can all better educate each other on helping friends who were experiencing symptoms of PTSD.

We were then excused to an early lunch after being told we would finish up the day as we normally would once lunch was over.

Abbi and I held hands at every opportune moment throughout the morning as Davis hung closely by, talking about what was going through his mind during Mr. Mack's speech. He also mentioned our bus driver's ongoing battle with his work regarding the damages done to our bus as a result of his evacuation efforts during the shooting. It was amazing anyone could be concerned with the financial impact so soon after the tragedy. To charge anyone for financial damage done as a result of his or her attempts save student lives, it just made no sense to me.

Abbi and I returned to gym class to find most everyone present outside Raymon and our gym teacher. Raymon wasn't injured in the shooting so we just assumed he wasn't ready to return to school yet. I sometimes got the feeling Raymon was an imitation of what he thought people wanted him to be. On the outside, he was tough and rebellious but deep down I imagined he was likely a sensitive guy, afraid of being rejected upon opening his true self up to the world around him.

The substitute gym teacher walked out and asked us all to do whatever we wanted to with the spare equipment they had. He then tossed basketballs, rackets, and other game equipment towards the center of the gym. Abbi and I weren't at all in the mood to play any sports or other games so we decided to just sit by and scribble pictures on each other's hands.

Not many students played much of anything during class, most the equipment just sat in the middle of the gym. We were all still processing the earlier speeches and dealing with how different everything felt. No matter what they said about or did to our school from that point, it would always remind us of death.

CHAPTER 9

The next day Abbi asked me to meet her after school.
She wanted to see me outside the church where she
had previously confronted me about the letter I wrote.
I suppose I could have been worried she was going to
talk about something dramatic, but Abbi had the
acquired a habit of not letting me down. I came to
trust her with my heart as it always felt safe in her
soft hands.

As I walked up to her she asked me "How much have
you missed me?" I replied, "How much does
someone in the middle of a desert long for water?"
She smiled and said "Well I missed you more than…"
She looked around for a second trying to think of
something only to laughed and give up on coming up
with a different analogy. She said, "I missed you to a
ridiculous extent too." She pulled me in close and
asked me another question, "Why haven't you kissed
me?" I smiled and replied "Well, you've kissed every
part of my face outside my lips, so I supposed I
should finally give something back." Her eyes lit up
and she gave me a huge smile.

Wrapping her hands around my neck, Abbi got up on
her tiptoes as a pulled herself towards me. She gave
me the softest kiss I had ever felt. A surge of
electricity shot between us. It felt like she was
melting into me, that we were, somehow, in that
moment, becoming one.

We continued to kiss as a tiny thought loomed in the side of my mind. I had passively noticed the wind around us ceasing in movement just after our lips connected, as if the moving air itself had to stop and soak in this moment. After quite a few minutes passed we began to walk home together.

Our walk took us longer than usual as we kept stopping at every other tree and building to kiss more. It was such an amazing feeling to be so important to someone, to be so loved.

As we approached Abbi's home we could hear loud music being played inside, reverberating through the walls. He father burst out the door; I imagine he saw us through one of his dirt-stained windows. Not caring that everyone around was about to get dunked into a massive tank of his emotional instability he screamed, "Abbigale! Where have you been?" He clenched a beer in his hand as he breathed in the same way I'd expect an angry bull with spears dangling from their bleeding back to. His inhaling seemed nearly as loud as his speech as he continued. "You got some damn chores to do! And I'm sick of you coming home late every other night!"

Abbi and I both knew most every time she was late, it was because she was sitting outside her house refusing to go in until she could determine whether or not her father was in a stable enough state to be around.

Abbi was squeezing my arm tightly as he continued to yell, "You think I won't abandon you just like your mother you little ungrateful brat? I raised you to show zero respect for me? Is that how I raised you?" Cars continued to pass by, unresponsive to her father's outbursts. Her father continued to scream seeming completely delusional and detached from the world around him. At that point I wasn't sure if it was more who he was or what he was using that made him become the monster he was. After a short while of his outburst I could see in the corner of my eye a police officer approach on foot. The officer, likely having seen this kind of behavior on a daily basis, now stood quietly in the distance with his work dog, just as silent as his master, looking on as well.

Her father continued to rant and throw objects lying outside at his own house, "Are you going to answer me? Are you going to say anything? Am I gonna have to drag you inside this house to get a response out of you?" After throwing a couple more rocks and bottles at his house he began to dance mockingly, "Because this whole world doesn't give a damn about you Abbigale! I could knock you right out and not a soul would care. No one cares about you but me! You disrespect me?" I opened my mouth to argue in her defense but Abbi pulled on my arm, physically insisting I stay silent.

Her father saw my mouth move and exploded on me, quickly shortening the distance between us as he spoke "What is it you punk? What do you have to say? Do you know what she is? Do you even know the first thing about this freak?" He violently shifted towards Abbi and began stumbling and reaching for her. Sounding deranged, he said "I'm gonna drag you in by your little rat tail Abbigale!" I quickly stepped in front of her. In complete shock, her father impulsively swung his beer at me; it collided with the side of my skull causing blood to pour out from underneath my hair. I remained standing but had trouble seeing, all I could hear was a deep grumbling tone accompanied by an irritating but subtle ringing.

I looked up slowly to see, with my blurred vision, the police dog dragging Abbi's dad away by his arm. From what I could make out the cop had no interest in calling the dog off. It was as if he enjoyed seeing people who commit unprovoked violence suffer an even greater opposing force as everyone knew it was over the moment the dog latched.

It had barely taken any time for Abbi to remove her jacket and press the soft interior against the side of my head. I could see her father's condition was not at all on her mind, she had chosen me, like I had chosen her, over not just one person or another but everyone.

30 minutes passed, and Abbi and I were both sitting on the ground as her father sat in the back of the K-9 SUV now parked in front of Abbi's house. The patrolman was waiting for an ambulance, emotionless. I knew it would be gullible of me to assume he had never seen anything like this; in fact it was probably a daily occurrence. Everyone gets numb to routine no matter how dramatic or strange. This officer had a look like he had seen this day come and go a hundred times before. Abbi's father was just another drunk, just another evolved ape throwing his life away.

When the ambulance arrived the patrolmen asked me if I wanted to press charges, I wasn't sure what to do until Abbi quickly leaned towards my ear, telling me that if I didn't, it would mean he could take out whatever anger he had on her after everyone had left, as he remained her legal guardian. Without further thought I made my choice and took the action that was in the best interest of her safety.

The officer asked Abbi if she wanted to have assistance with her living situation while they dealt with her father, she replied that she would stay with me. "Are you sure about that? Kid's going to need some stitches, might be a little groggy for a few days with that head injury." She replied, "It may as well have been me, and that's all the more reason for me to stay with him. I'm not going anywhere." He nodded as the ambulance pulled up, briefing the driver, he then ensured he had everything he needed to process his paperwork, and left the area with Abbi's father in custody.

The ambulance workers stitched me up then and there. While they were finishing up, Abbi called us a taxi, which shortly after returned us to my home.

Abbi and I rested on my bed covers still wearing our shoes and everything. My mind was too distracted by what had happened when we came in to worry about dirty blankets. Breaking the silence Abbi said, "You're the most loving and selfless person I've ever known." I still felt conflicted about so many things outside Abbi but I didn't want to ruin her compliment so I replied "But you forgot to include yourself, Abbi." She smiled doubtfully. I stared into her eyes, and she tried to look back, but was struggling with emotions rapidly overtaking her. She began tearing up and said, "Well James, whatever love I have, it's all for you." Tears began to fall down her face, "I love you too," I said. She started crying and pulled herself tightly against me. "I love you," she whispered under her breath continuing to cry.

Together, we drifted gently into a warm sleep.

CHAPTER 10

The next morning I was surprised Davis didn't leap up to greet me as I walked on the bus with Abbi. We sat across from him but he just looked out his window, surrounding himself in a silent gloom while paying us no attention. "Hey Davis, how are you today?" I asked, Davis replied without turning towards me, "Why don't you have a car? You're 17, only losers like me ride the bus." Abbi gave me a look of concern. Though Abbi didn't know Davis too well yet, she understood him to be a happier person; neither of us expected Davis to say something so negative. I responded to Davis, "Not everyone has a white picket fence life Davis, some people have to ride the bus." Davis turned angrily and spoke as he pierced me with the most intense glare I had ever seen, "You don't think I know that? You should get a job! Buy your own car! What are you even doing with your life?"

I sat back, giving up on changing his mood and thought to myself "Happiness, as far as I care, can't be acquired through any means if love is not involved." If I got a job on top of school, I'd have barely any time to spend with Abbi. I needed her more than anything and I thought Davis knew this. Davis was probably just upset over everything that had happened recently and this was his way of coping.

Trying to close the conversation on a less negative note I said, "Well buddy, I'm here if you need me!" with the same tone he always used on me. He rolled his eyes, scoffed and scooted closer to his window. Abbi remained next to me, running her fingers over the hairs on my hand. It was such a positive distraction.

Later that morning I found myself in my History class staring at a very nervous Mr. Hanson. "You all realize the President of the United freaking States is going to be here right?" he asked the class. Most the students looked confused, as we were not briefed when exactly we would see him.

A voice erupted as our classroom door was swiftly pushed open. "The President of the United freaking States is about to arrive ladies and gentlemen," said a large man wearing a black suit. Mr. Hanson laughed nervously over the fact that, what we soon realized was a member of the Secret Service, had overheard him. Mr. Hanson turned to the class and in a rushed tone said "Alright, think before you ask the President anything, no stupid questions!" Another voice came from outside the door "You're right Mr. Hanson, there are no stupid questions." We all froze to see it was the President who had spoken.

As he walked in the room I quickly realized he was much taller than I had assumed from watching TV. The President centered himself in the room as the

Secret Service asked Mr. Hanson to take a seat at his desk.

Four members of the USSS stood behind the President as he began to speak, "I'm not here to bring a dark cloud into this room. I want to be uplifting, to be helpful, and I want all of you to feel like you can say whatever you like, without any fear of criticism or repercussion" Chris Jenkins, the class clown, blurted out "Why are you such a D-Bag?" Most everyone in the class sat in shock as Mr. Hanson violently lurched up like a frantic animal yelling in a high-pitched tone "Chris! How dare you disrespect the..." "Mr. Hanson." the President interrupted, "Thank you." A USSS member then asked Mr. Hanson to return to his seat.

The President walked over to Chris, pulling his own pants slightly back so he could crouch. "Now you may feel I am what you said, a D-Bag, but you should know to address me as President D-Bag as I, and many Americans, believe I earned the title of President."

Chris, now shaking and not knowing what to say let out a nervous and horribly awkward chuckle. The President smiled and returned to the front of the room as he said "Now what other questions do you all have for me?" Literally everyone in class aside from Chris raised their hand. The President looked directly at me and said "James Patrick, the boy who nearly saved the day, what is your question?" I replied, "You know who I am?" He responded, "I've read up on this school and the recent events quite a bit. How are your feet healing up?" I was overwhelmed but I had to keep it together so I quickly replied, "Really well actually, the ambulance guys did an amazing job getting the glass and dirt out." The President followed with "That's wonderful to hear, what was your question?" I replied, "I just wanted to know how you feel about the things people call you, in the news and around the world."

The President gave a slightly sad smile and replied "I cannot, and do not want to control what people say about me. All I can really fully control is what I myself am saying and doing. I find myself repeatedly stating that I came into office with the best intentions, and I continue to lead as President with those very same intentions. Some decisions I have to make aren't always fair to me, my family or many people around the world, but sometimes your only options lie between the end of a slipknot or the blade a guillotine, and that's the burden I chose to carry." The class paused for a few seconds and then all at once everyone but Chris & myself raised their hands again.

One of the USSS members spoke up "Mr. President we need to move on." The President lifted his hand and said to the class "I want you all to know there are going to be some major changes around your school.

I've approved a budget shift that will help fund significant renovations and an effective security program that will promote a safer environment for everyone here."

"I will not stand by and do nothing when these incidents occur. So I'm doing what any responsible person in my position would do to make you all feel safer in this learning environment." He then smiled as the USSS opened the door behind him. "Thank you all, and Chris, remember our talk, ok?" Chris remained speechless as the President walked out.

Mr. Hanson then stood up while looking at Chris as if he had just slapped Mr. Hanson's mother right in front of him. Mr. Hanson maintained his glare as he walked to the front of class.

Mr. Hanson sighed deeply and looked down at the floor, he then asked, "Did anyone else almost pass out?" The class erupted with laughter as the teacher wiped sweat from his forehead with the towel he used as a white board eraser. The towel smeared ink all over his forehead, which made us all laugh even harder. Unfortunately I was faced with the reality that he would blame his humiliation on me if I did not tell him right away, as my next period still required I act as a Teachers' Assistant for him.

The first thing Abbi said to me when I met with her later that day in gym class was "So it looks like Mrs.

Stanley's getting a new desk." I replied "The president?" "Yep, he met with you guys too?" I nodded and she added "In other news, Jason has been hitting on me, not sure what to do about it." I replied concerned "Like just flirting, or is it heavy?" She answered, "I think the whole saving our lives thing went to his head. He just grabbed my butt in class after the President left the room." I went silent.

Trying to reassure me she said "I yelled at him not do it again." I replied, "Did you talk to the teacher?" She answered "Mrs. Stanley saw I was uncomfortable and said she would give him detention if he tried to do it again." I loved that she did everything I would have done, leaving no room for me to imagine potential alternatives to what she felt about Jason's chauvinistic act. I smiled slightly and said "Well, thank you for telling me…" She interrupted "What about you? Any girls grabbing your butt these days?" I replied with a slight smile, "Nope, guess my butt just isn't as good looking as yours." She squealed and hugged me as the substitute walked in and blew his whistle.

"All right everyone let's play some badminton!" the sub said, pronouncing everything as it was spelled. Raymon responded "Don't you mean bad-mitten?" The teacher replied "I didn't Ray-man, is that ok with you?" Now angered, he responded, "It's Ray-mon!" The sub laughed and said "Alright everyone, do you want to see Ray-man vs. your sub in bad-min-ton?" A lot of us screamed "Yeah!" and so the game ensued.

Raymon seemed to get hit with the birdie more than the actual racket did. We kept laughing because he was trying so hard to look cool but kept failing repeatedly and as a result, looked completely goofy. After the teacher had scored on him for the 10th time Raymon threw down his racket. The teacher loudly asked, "So is that game? No more bad-min-ton?" trying to sound tough Raymon screamed, "This is a sissy game anyway!" Someone watching yelled to everyone "Uh oh watch out he might try to shoot us too!" We all went silent; one girl jumped up and walked off in a hurry. I could see she was holding her cries in until she could get out of the room.

Raymon angrily looked over at the person who made the comment. The individual who yelled put their head down. They were obviously trying to avoid being pierced by Raymon's glare. Raymon then furiously walked off, throwing a tantrum by kicking a garbage can while pulling off his shirt as he passed through the boys' locker room entrance.

"Alright everyone, pick a partner and start playing!" the teacher said just before following Raymon into the locker room.

Naturally Abbi was on my team and we played against a couple of people who were equally unenthusiastic about the sport so we basically just stood around talking about how dorky our uniforms were and basically anything we could to keep our minds preoccupied.

Later that night at dinner, we had to put together a makeshift chair for Rick as Abbi was still staying with us. My mom began to talk about their move "So Rick let me know he's happy to help cover your food, utilities etcetera while you stay here in the condo." she said, Abbi and I looked at each other happily and hugged excited that it was confirmed. Abbi and I didn't have to move anywhere.

My mom continued, "Your sister is going to come with us." I looked at my sister and asked, "What's up sis?" She just pushed food around on her plate and mumbled, "It's whatever. I don't want to talk about it." My mom gave me a look that I should just drop it, so I did.

Abbi squeezed my hand; she was still smiling widely at me. I was pretty overwhelmed with what this all meant as well. One of the greatest pending burdens hovering over my head had been removed from my life completely. However ridiculous it sounds, knowing I could be separated from Abbi, to me, was the equivalent of a doctor telling me I might have cancer, only to reveal later, it was nothing. I felt like I was getting my life back, without ever really having it taken away in the first place.

After dinner, Abbi and I cuddled in bed while listening to some of her favorite bands. She would sing along to the songs, knowing most the words, as I just kept my eyes closed, paying close attention to how her skin felt pressed against mine.

In that room alone with her, I often found myself feeling like nothing else mattered. She gave all my senses something to devour to the point where I began to feel like the rest of the world barely existed at all.

I fell asleep listening to the sound of her beautiful voice, softly singing.

CHAPTER 11

Ms. Robertson, essentially the best therapist our tiny school budget could offer, had called me in her office, just as she had many students before me, to get an update on how we were doing with all things considered. She greeted me in her usual way, slightly awkward, but attempting to seem sincere. I suppose it was hard giving it her all when she, and many of her coworkers, had been underappreciated and underpaid by her employers from day one.

"Are you still with Abbi?" she firmly asked out of nowhere. I replied, "Yes." She said "I'll be talking to her later today, how are things between you two?" I answered again "Good, a lot of good things are happening." Ms. Robertson looked skeptical and changed the subject. "So, you ran through the school, barefoot during the shooting?" I replied, "Yes, I was looking for Abbi." Again, Ms. Robertson gave me a look of frustration and disbelief.

Picking up on her consistent negative physical body language and verbal tone I asked "Is there something you're not telling me Ms. Robertson?" She replied, "I can't really tell you anything, not legally, as far as I know. I just hope you take my original advice. Be careful, think twice about what you're doing, that's all I can say." I looked down at the floor trying to figure out what she was talking about. "So you're not at all depressed?" she asked. I replied "No, not that I know of." She then asked "Not that you know of?" I replied, "No, I'm not depressed." She nodded and said "Well that's, of course, good." Ms. Robertson walked over to her window overlooking the football field out back. She mumbled something in a low tone I couldn't make out and then said loudly "You can send the next person in James." I was surprised by how cold Ms. Robertson was acting towards me, but was happy to leave.

Later in gym class, we were hoping to see Mr. Mack, though we all knew it was unreasonable to expect such a fast recovery. Abbi was wearing one of my shirts when she first got in, smiling happily before she disappeared in the locker room.

When she returned, I asked her "Did you talk to Ms. Robertson yet?" Abbi replied without hesitation "Yes." I then asked, "What do you think of her?" She replied, "I think… she's a guidance counselor. What am I supposed to think?" I was put off by her hesitation and by what I perceived to be an evasive response.

I paid close attention to Abbi's voice and movements. Her tone was abnormally higher pitched when she spoke of Ms. Robertson, that small detail stood out like a skyscraper piercing the clouds of an otherwise small town. To me, she seemed… "You're psycho analyzing me again, aren't you James?" she asked, interrupting my thoughts. I replied, feeling foolish,

"Yes, sorry." She then replied, "The world is full of critics, I don't want to fear judgment from you." I understood her wishes all too well, but I felt justified in looking further into what may have really been going on. I replied, "I was just asking about the guidance counselor. Your response might be revealing that there is in fact something I'm not yet aware of going on. Something I should probably know about." "James, stop" she said loudly, I decided to back off. I didn't want to upset her, especially with the remaining school day pending. Having conflict looming over my head while trying to focus on class was unfortunately a nearly impossible and stress-saturated task for me, so I had to just let it go for now.

We arrived home later that day to find no one was home. Abbi and I made dinner for each other and once we finished eating, she asked me if I wanted to sit in the bathroom while she showered. My shower curtains were thick and non-transparent so while it would seem like a huge step in our relationship, it kind of wasn't.

She started the shower water and closed the door while I cleaned the kitchen. Moments later she yelled out "James! I'm ready!" and closed the door again to keep the heat in the bathroom.

Walking into the bathroom I could see the curtain was fully closed. I said, "Hey did you want to talk?" She replied, "Yeah, I'm sorry for putting up a wall earlier.

That was weird of me right?" I said, "That's ok. I mean, sometimes providing space is the best way of to create more potential for personal growth." Ignoring the overly philosophical nature of my response she replied, "I love you James, and I don't want to hide anything from you." I said, "I love you too... I know this may sound boring, but I've basically shared every major story in my life with you already." She replied, "I know... it's really nice to be with someone who I can actually trust. No painful surprises." I paused and thought for a way to lighten the mood. I then said, "Of course, it takes a much more mysterious person than me to be deceptive you know? I'm kind of like a window that way." She remained silent.

After a couple minutes of thinking, she spoke up, saying, "Ms. Robertson hates me." Hearing this, I felt reassured in my earlier suspicions. I could now see it was safe to continue digging. I asked, "Why would she hate you?" She went silent for a moment. "I used to see her a lot, I had... or... I donno... I just struggled a lot before I met you." She said. Thinking about what she was saying I felt overwhelmed, it was the same sensation I experienced every time she reminded me how important I was to her. I felt so unworthy, like I was given a gift intended for royalty, not someone as insignificant as myself.

I replied trying to encourage Abbi "Whatever you were going through before we were together… I mean… I wouldn't say I love you if I wasn't willing to stand by you through everything." She listened and stood in silence for a short time after. I imagined her mind racing to piece everything together. I think she was trying to create a definitive picture of who we were together. I felt she wanted some simple visual aid to sum it all up; she wanted to give it a name. She had all the stitches, fabric, and stuffing, was she sewing it all together?

Looking away from the shower towards the bathroom door, I heard the sound of the curtains opening beside me. "Look at me James." she said in a more collected tone. I looked over at her to see her completely naked body standing before me.

"Do you see why a school therapist would have a problem with me?" she asked. I was in awe. My heart was suddenly pounding in my chest and I could barely think clearly. I was consumed with thoughts of how perfect she looked, how everything I had imagined was a poor imitation of what reality was now showing me.

"I… see…" I said, struggling to speak. She asked "What James? I'm broken? I'm wrecked? I'm worthless now?" I quickly replied, "I see perfection, nothing else." She stood before me frozen, her arm still holding the curtains back. Staring at me I could see what I had said was racing through her mind. In a soft tone she asked "Is this really perfection James?" as she began pointing out the scars on her body from self-harm, but before she could get past the first few, I began kissing every scar within my sight.

Like a dam rapidly cracking open she began to pour out as I kissed her marks, I continued kissing despite her whimpers, I knew this meant everything to her. I wanted to show her how much I loved every part of her, so I kissed and kissed as her body shivered, still so warm, but consumed by sadness and the fallout of a now retreating fear. I slowly made my way up to her lips and looked deep into her eyes.

I was still completely clothed, but had stepped entirely into the shower. She and I kissed heavily as a held her naked body against me. In an instant, we were interrupted with a soul-shattering thunderous bang on our home's entrance door. Abbi looked away and then back at me with a panicked expression.

I whispered in her ear "Don't worry, I left a distraction, you can slip into my room safely." Abbi gave a slight smiled and nodded. In the background my mom let out a loud and sarcastic "Oh great!" having seen exactly what I hoped she would near the entrance. Abbi wrapped a towel around her and, without hesitation, darted across the hall to my room.

I remained in the bathroom, now pulling off my clothes to shower and avoid further confrontation. "Who knocked the trash over?" my mom screamed as I quietly laughed to myself. It was ironic that I knocked it over considering I was supposed to clean the kitchen, but when Abbi called me into the bathroom I figured my mom might not be happy with me being in there with her. She was just another parent horrified by the idea of teen pregnancy.

As I finished my shower, I could hear my mom muttering in the kitchen about how she was tired of cleaning up after people. "Sorry mom!" I yelled, and she replied "You're lucky I love you otherwise this would not fly!" I replied, "I know! I love you too! I'll vacuum the whole house later to make up for it!" I said as I closed my door.

Upon my door latching closed, Abbi leapt on me, wrapping her pajama-covered legs around me. My towel fell around my ankles as I dropped my soaked clothes to hold her.

She looked down to see me fully naked and laughed. I quickly pointed out in a positive tone how awkward her reaction was, "Because that's what a guy wants to hear." She replied "No! I'm just surprised that happened, sorry to knock your towel off." She jumped off and kissed me quickly on the lips only to drop down to grab my towel.

As she rose back up slowly, she stopped for a nerve-racking moment at my waist. I said "Hey!" and she laughed innocently, quickly wrapping the towel around my waist. Abbi then stood up completely to continue kissing me.

That night as we cuddled in bed I said to her "You know... you really do look amazing naked." She laughed and said "Shut up!" laughing some more. I replied, "No, I'm serious, you're so perfect. Every part of you looks better than I could ever imagine." She looked back at me as I rested behind her. "Kiss me," she said.

We began kissing heavily once again, this time sliding off each other's clothes. Though we didn't try to go any further than just being physically close. We would lie there, kissing and loving the feeling of each other, without any barriers.

We fell asleep in each other's arms, our hair a mess, so comfortable we didn't care about anything but being together.

That night I felt I was closer to her than anyone in my entire life.

CHAPTER 12

Abbi was still asleep when I woke the next morning. It was still early so I just relaxed and watched her sleep for a while. At some point to my surprise Abbi said with her eyes still closed "Why are you staring at me James?" Pleasantly caught off guard I said "Oh my god!" and started to laugh. She replied, "I got you creeper!" now laughing with me. I felt so silly but replied, "I don't regret it. You look so beautiful." She pulled the blankets up to rest just under her eyes laughing in disbelief.

Just then, a knock sounded off on the door and my mom said "Hey, you're not going to school today, you're helping me pack!" We both replied, saying, "Ok mom!" My heart fluttered hearing Abbi call my mom, well, "Mom". I looked at Abbi in disbelief. She looked back and said "What? She could be my mom one day." Seeing her say that made my eyes feel like they were about to water, I was so happy to see how serious she was about us being together.

Abbi and I got dressed so we could help my mom. I carried most of the boxes and smaller furniture by myself to the truck because Rick wasn't going to be there until later that night. It also made me feel good about myself, as my mom and Abbi would compliment how strong they thought I was every time I walked out with something heavy.

Quite a few hours into working my mom called Davis over to help after school was over for him. Davis seemed kind of upset with me still, but he was at least smiling more, which I was happy to see.

My mom asked if I could pick up more box tape from the store, she knew I loved driving her car, or any car for that matter, so she tossed me the keys. Abbi was going to go, but my mom asked her to stay behind and help pack up her room.

"Davis, want to ride in a car with a total loser?" I asked jingling the keys. Davis responded "Yeah, of course I do buddy." smiling slightly but not sounding as happy as he normally did.

As we drove down the road, Davis asked me a lot of questions about Abbi, like about how serious we were and if I thought she was the one. He then asked "But you don't... like... you don't ever think about other people romantically?" I replied, "No, she's literally the center of my world Davis." He looked really upset by this. I asked "You don't like Abbi?" and he replied, "No, I like her just fine."

We approached the store and got out. As we walked in, he made fun of my shoes, likely trying to get away from the awkward conversation we had about Abbi. Once we were in the store he started wrapping tape around his head, contorting his face while dancing around looking totally freaky. I said, "Hey, I have to pay for that." he then turned to me looking completely goofy as he mimicked what I said with his warped tape face. "Hey, I got to, duh, pay, duh, for that, duh!" he said with his amazing comedic timing. I immediately began laughing hysterically only to shortly after realize I was the only one in the store who was even remotely amused.

Walking up to the cashier, Davis still with tape still all over his face, I said "Can you also ring up this... whole thing?" making a hand gesture at the various tape rolls attached to his face. The cashier remained disinterested but complied using their remote scanner. Davis smiled putting his arms up like a ballerina, spinning as they scanned the tape hanging from his head. We giggled as they gave us our bags and we left.

On the way out, Davis wasn't done yet, he turned to everyone in the store and screamed "Hi ho silver lady mammy poppy sickle!" His antics made no sense yet still caused me to laugh even harder than I had before. "Come on Davis!" I screamed as I headed into the parking lot. "Okie dokie captain derp!" he screamed back.

As we drove back home, despite having to pull the tape off his face in a painful fashion, Davis seemed much happier. It was nice to get his mind off the number of things I imagined were bothering him.

After a few more hours we had finished packing up everything my mom was taking with her. My sister was pretty unhelpful the whole time, mostly just moping around the house, barely speaking at all.

I approached my mom to ask about her, "Mom, why is Lisa so bummed out?" I said. My mom stood up and said, "Close the door." I closed the door only to ask again; this time my mom answered, "A boy she liked, Matthew, died in the shooting." I had only heard about him in passing, but it became clear my sister wasn't just giving her heart to every other guy she met like I had assumed. My mom continued, "She said everything at the school reminds her of him, that's why she's coming with us." I thought for a moment and replied "But she's a senior, won't that mean she has to graduate late?" My mom answered, "She'll do what she has to, they'll hopefully recognize her current grades and transfer them, but either way she's done with this place."

I sighed and left the room without poking any further into my sisters business. As I walked back into my room I saw Abbi sitting on the bed. "Abbi, want to drop off Davis with me?" She smiled and said "Yep." I called out for Davis and we all got into to my mom's car.

Once again, Davis didn't seem too comfortable with Abbi, him having to take the back seat I'm sure didn't help either, but he still tried to make polite

conversation. We dropped him off and waited to see him make it all the way inside. Before he closed the door he screamed, "You look like a couple of stalkers! God!" We laughed and he grinned really big only to slam the door.

As we drove back home Abbi asked if we could stop by a nearby park. I replied, noting that it was getting late, but she said she had something she wanted to experience with me. Pulling up to the park, she pointed out a specific spot and I slowed to stop as I could get to where she wanted.

Abbi got out and rested on the warm hood of my mom's car. I said, "How about that? I didn't take you for the star-gazing type." She smiled and replied, "It's not just stars. This is everything. You could look at every part of the Earth and you still wouldn't see as much as you would if you just looked up at the night sky. Looking at the universe has always helped me escape this tiny little life of mine." I smiled, once again comforted by almost everything her mind had to share with me. I slid on the hood next to her and looked up at the stars as well.

"What if stars were like birds, and they took craps on us…" I said as she interrupted with a sarcastic laugh, "Stop, just stop, you're stupid." I laughed and out of nowhere asked a question that oddly surprised us both, "Do you think we'll have kids some day?" She tilted her head and responded jokingly, "Whoa, too fast. I just wanted to look at the entire universe with you, that's all." I laughed again and teased her by saying, "You're right, no kids." She sat up, "No! I want kids." I smiled having gotten exactly the response I wanted, I then said with a huge grin, "Gotcha". She became more serious and asked "You do?" I answered somewhat cryptically, "Every significant moment in my life, I want to share with you." She smiled and leaned in to kiss me. She then spoke under her cherry-smelling breath "Every significant moment to come in my life will be significant because of you James." I was overwhelmed with emotion; since Abbi and I began dating I felt more purpose, more value in my life, than I had ever known.

Abbi and I looked at the stars a little longer and headed home to spend yet another night in each other's arms.

CHAPTER 13

Christmas was closing in on us, so Abbi found herself often talking about her excitement for what gifts she was going to get me. I was just happy that I would be spending the holiday with her exclusively as my mom had already moved out and planned to spend the holidays with Rick up on the ski slopes.

It was our last day of school before winter break, which pretty much guaranteed us freezing as we waited for the bus. To my surprise, Davis welcomed us both as we climbed on. He shouted, "If it isn't Mr. and Mrs. Santy Clause here to bring joy and love to everyone!" We both smiled and I could see Abbi was quickly becoming just as enchanted by Davis as I was.

Abbi sat down with me only to quickly huddle next to me for warmth. "Did you slip on the ice on the way over Mr. Clause?" Davis asked. I replied "No ho ho!" and grinned. He said, "No but really, I'm surprised they didn't cancel school, its kind of super crazy out." The bus driver screamed "Sorry about the lack of heat, they gave me a pretty crappy bus! They said I couldn't handle the other busses or some junk like that." Davis leapt up, shouting back "We love you Mr. Bus driver! You saved our lives!" The driver then asked "Oh yeah, what's my name?" Davis replied almost instantly, "Well what's my name?" The bus driver responded, "I asked first!" Davis said again

"Well I'll just call you superhero for now!" The bus driver laughed as Davis sat back down giggling.

As the bus pulled up to our school we could see the early stages of what would likely be heavy construction. I asked the bus driver what was going on and he replied, "Well, ever since that shooting you guys have become quite the symbol of hope for the country. Pretty sure the President has a hand in paying all these workers double what they'd usually make to get all these renovations done by the time winter break is over."

As we stepped onto the cement walkway just outside the bus we could hear large chunks of salt crumbling under our feet. Davis busted out with more antics. "Whoa! This salt is super slippery!" he said as he stumbled around like a drunken uncle on ice.

Abbi and I said goodbye to Davis as he did another goofy impression while we walked away. I hugged Abbi and kissed her before we also parted ways. As I turned away she slipped a note in my pocket. I turned and said with a smile "Really?" She responded, "I know, but I wrote it while you slept last night, so what'cha gonna do?"

Walking off to class, I reflected on the lingering feeling I had, like I was living a life that was too good for me. It was as if everything had worked out despite me having an underlying sensation that I had yet to earn my happiness. But I suppose that comes with the constant self-inflicted reminder of how small I am in the world.

To me, love was really the only thing that kept me going, I felt like someone who had swam too far into the ocean but somehow found a piece of driftwood to cling to. For me, that one piece of wood wasn't just some random object in the ocean... it was my life. This simple piece of wood represented my capacity to love and my only hope of staying alive. Abbi didn't just give me hope, but also a promise that so long as I had her I would never slip back into the numb existence I was living in before.

I sat in Washington State History class and tried to open the note Abbi wrote me but Mr. Hanson immediately gave me a dirty look. He then lurched up out of his seat, wiped his forehead and walked over putting his hand out to receive the note. "You know there's no note reading in this class, give it to me James" he said without any sign of compassion. Mr. Hanson was mostly a nice guy, but he rarely joked around with class rules, I thought he wouldn't be as hard on me as I was his TA next period, but I was clearly wrong. I had to think fast so I replied saying "Sorry I have to go to the bathroom." I stood up quickly and walked out of the class as Mr. Hanson blurted out "I said give me the note James!" Ignoring his command, I pushed my way into the restroom down the hall and locked myself in a stall.

I opened the note to find the following: "James, I'm laying here next to you, ironically watching you sleep despite my previous jokes about you doing the same. I want to talk to you so badly right now, but I don't want to wake you, especially not with what I have to say.

I keep telling you I don't want anything to be hidden between us and I mean that. You haven't asked me about what I initially spoke to you about behind the church regarding the letter you wrote me...

I told you about friends that had taken advantage of me, and later I showed you my many scars, but I haven't told you everything James. You should hear everything. You deserve to know… everything.

Ms. Robertson was supportive of me when I came to her about being raped. She even helped me make sure the boys responsible saw their day in court and were expelled from this school.

I'm having a really hard time even writing this, but, James, I was going to… as a result of what those boys did... I became pregnant. I told Ms. Robertson and found out right after that she is extremely pro-life, and I mean extremely. I told her I didn't want to give them the satisfaction of bringing their child into this world, but she kept saying I shouldn't punish another person for the actions of their biological father.

I was dating Seth at the time. I didn't tell Seth who had raped me because I knew he was psychotic but I still cared about him and didn't want him to throw his life away by doing something he couldn't take back. Obviously, I couldn't change the path he was going down. He saw my behavior change as the pregnancy progressed. After a while of seeing the state I was in, he asked me to admit to him what he suspected. I refused to tell him anything and told him to leave it alone so he threw me against the wall and demanded I admit what I was hiding. Once I confessed I was pregnant he, without hesitation, punched me repeatedly in the stomach. I was sobbing and he just kept yelling at me, telling me everything was my fault. Despite me trying to protect my stomach he would just pull my hands away so he could punch me again and again.

My father walked in on Seth yelling at me and he demanded Seth leave but Seth refused. I screamed at Seth that we were over from the floor where I was laying… I kept telling him it was over. With every breath I could manage, I made sure he knew I didn't want to see him again. It was the only power I had and I used it to fight back.

My father was threatening Seth saying he was going to get his gun but Seth just kept screaming about how he was being punished for saving my life as he saw it, so my father grabbed him and physically forced him to leave.

My father drove me to the hospital, I suppose the only time he can act like a good guy is when there's an even worse person around. They gave me pain medication and not too long after, it became clear to me that I was no longer pregnant. I felt like everything was my fault.

Shortly after this all happened I started cutting myself. I hated myself more than anyone. Every time I looked in the mirror, I saw someone who was broken, damaged beyond repair." I had to stop reading for a moment to collect myself. Tears were falling down my face. I imagined her eyes vividly in my mind; the ocean wall of tears I had seen behind her eyes and the sadness I felt from her was being laid out right in front of me. She wrote about her life falling apart and, the more she explained, the more everything seemed to come together.

I continued reading.

"I went to Ms. Robertson with all this information and she turned her back on me completely. She was convinced that I got Seth to punch me so I would lose the baby and she was clearly holding me responsible for a life that I couldn't... she could barely even look at me.

My father treated me differently after it all happened as well… he too acted like I was at fault for how things wound up, just like Ms. Robertson, despite me never asking for any of it. I have no idea if I would have gone through with the pregnancy. I felt like I was willing to adopt them out once they were born, but Seth didn't ask me what I wanted.

James... I'm sure at this point you may be wondering why I was with Seth when we started talking. The pregnancy was over a year before I even talked to you, so obviously I got back together with him... It's really hard to explain, but I'll do my best.

The reality is, I had no one left. I couldn't talk to Ms. Robertson about my cutting or depression, I couldn't talk to my Dad... all I had was Seth, who didn't even have to ask for me to take him back. I freely went to him because he was the only person who was even willing to talk to me. I felt like no one else felt I was worth anything. Despite him making me feel horrible both emotionally and physically, he at least acknowledged my existence beyond the few words I could get from anyone else. After everything, I felt like he was all I deserved.

That's when I noticed you, staring at me in class. I didn't think you would ever give me a chance once you discovered me, but you did. You pulled me away from the horrible life I had found myself living and made me feel happier than I knew possible. My life before I knew you seems more and more like some long, painful nightmare. It was a nightmare that I don't have to worry about slipping into anymore.

I trust you James, please... I can't... I'm sorry." I dropped the note, staring only for a moment at it in my lap. The more I read, the more I wanted to hold her. I just wanted to be there to take her away before any of these things could have ever happened.

Without a second thought I crammed the note into my pocket and began walking quickly towards Abbi's 1st period class.

Approaching her class door I aggressively pulled it open and walked across the room towards Abbi. Her teacher screamed "Excuse me son!" and one of the students yelled out "Oh God! Not again!" I ignored both of them grabbing Abbi by the center of her back and back of her leg lifting her up to wrap her legs around me. She said, her voice shaking, "James?" I sat her on her desk and pulled her neck towards me, kissing her deeply and passionately, ignoring everything but her.

"Unacceptable!" the teacher screamed angrily as the class erupted with "Oooohhhh!" just like I had heard in the earlier fistfights. It was the first time I felt anything positive from hearing that sound. I continued to deeply kiss Abbi sticking my tongue in her mouth, she sucked on my tongue matching my passion. She bit my lip and I bit hers. We were disgusting and beautiful together in the same instance, showing no shame for our raw passion. The teacher nearly lost it as they screamed, "Are you looking to get suspended? This is a classroom!"

I pulled slightly back from Abbi and asked "Through everything?" She replied with a huge smile on her face, "Absolutely everything." I then grabbed her again by the back of her leg and middle of her back to sit her down again. I turned to the door and walked out. I could hear the class continued to react in an uproar over what they had just witnessed as I waked away. Off in the distance behind me I could hear the teacher screaming outside their classroom "Is anyone going to do anything about this?" but he was the only staff member around, class was still in session.

Walking back into Mr. Hanson's class I was greeted by a bitter and sarcastic tone "Did you have a good squat?" I ignored him grinning as I returned to my seat.

During the TA period after, Mr. Hanson got a phone call and looked immediately in my direction. "James made out with a girl in her class?" he said. Mr. Hanson stared at me and continued, "Well, he said he was going to the bathroom." He looked up at me while covering up the phone and asked in a loud whispery tone "What exactly did she write you?"

before I gave any response he looked back as if listening to the phone and said to them "Never mind, anyway, long story short I think this place could benefit from a little distraction don't you?" The voice on the phone sounded outraged so he continued, "Well, you may as well just call winter break his suspension because it's the last day anyway." The person on the other end went silent and hung up.

Mr. Hanson looked up at me and said, "You really are something strange kid." I smiled, having just seen a glimmer of a real human being inside Mr. Hanson for the first time that day and replied, "Thanks for sticking up for me." He then said, "Consider us even." I smiled and returned to grading the papers I was assigned and he added "Let's just hope I don't get beat up after class for that like you did though." I laughed and he chuckled to himself.

CHAPTER 14

Every second felt like ten, but finally gym class had arrived. Abbi approached me, talking as she came close, "Thank you for the display Romeo, now the whole school is talking about us." I replied, "One of the best decisions I ever made." She wrapped her arms around me and whispered in my ear "I can't wait till we get home." Once again, stunning explosions illuminated my mind. My body felt like it was being lifted off the ground, I felt untouchable. I kissed her deeply as a voice interrupted "Hey! Aren't you suspended kid?" It was the substitute gym teacher.

I replied, "I… guess I am?" He said "See you after winter break, get out of here." I looked at Abbi and she said, "I guess we won't have to wait." She began to follow me out. The sub saw us both leaving and said "Hey! Abbigale, you have to stay." She replied while smiling as she continued walking out, "What are you going to do? Suspend me?" The teacher stood there looking dumbfounded. As the doors slammed behind us, he feared the rest of the class would follow suit. He quickly turned to the remaining students and said "Don't you think about it! I will call your parents!" They responded with a disappointed "Aww" as he proceeded by throwing out sports equipment for them to half-heartedly utilize.

Infatuated with one another, Abbi and I struggled to make it to our front door. We left our jackets in the hallway and were kissing heavily even as I turned the key to let us in.

She jumped on me and wrapped her legs around my waist. I slammed the door behind us, kissing her as I carried her to the bedroom. Without hesitation she pulled her shirt and bra off revealing her naked breasts and continued to kiss me. We collided with the bed as if we were one, silently crashing together, our hands running up and down each other's body. She pulled off her pants as I removed my shirt. Before I even had it completely off I could feel her kissing my stomach as she removed my pants.

We were completely naked in bed, sliding our bodies together. I whispered in her ear "Hang on to something" so she immediately grabbed onto the bed frame as I made my way down past her breasts slowing as I passed her hips, tasting her skin every inch of the way.

She moaned over and over, many times softly, with a sense of warmth in her voice. Other times her voice would surge intensity into the room, sounding so perfect, as if I were listening to an orchestra hitting every note with precise execution. I didn't stop; I couldn't stop devouring her till she began gushing and screaming wildly beyond control. It was only then I returned to look deeply into her eyes. She was begging for me to go even further. I firmly grabbed her waist and slid my hips slowly up her now soaking legs. She greeted me as if she had been waiting her whole life, digging her fingers into my back, scraping her nails across my skin as she moaned, her body connecting perfectly with mine, moving in sync, experiencing pure ecstasy.

For the rest of the day, we made love more than anything else, having only a few moments to drink water and recover. We couldn't make it more than 20 minutes without finding ourselves clashing together once more, losing ourselves completely to our desires.

As the day passed us by, we found ourselves absorbed into each other perfectly, and we both knew from that point on, we could never truly be apart. Every piece of me now had a small part of her sewn in with a thread stronger than the pieces themselves.

CHAPTER 15

Winter break came to a close; Abbi and I had spent our entire vacation exploring everything we desired of each other. We returned to school as happy as we could be.

As we walked through the doors hand in hand, a significantly remodeled interior was there to greet us. Excited teachers walked around with smiles of satisfaction on their faces, no doubt in response to the significant improvements to their own classrooms let alone the entire school.

"Sir, can you remove all metal items?" a man dressed as a security guard said to me. I felt surprised but that feeling quickly left me when I had remembered what the President said during his visit to the school regarding his dedication to improving security.

Removing everything from our pockets, Abbi and I were allowed to pass through. We waited as they searched through our backpacks and, shortly after, found ourselves parting ways once more only this time, despite our bodies being apart, we remained connected on an entirely new level. We could both feel it and it offered comfort in a way we never knew.

Making love to Abbi ignited my senses and thoughts beyond what I knew to be possible. We awakened a new plane of existence in ourselves emotionally, physically, intellectually and spiritually. We found ourselves living in a state of mind we hadn't imagined before, discovering what could only be found between people who passionately love each other. I found myself lost in the memory of us together, how she looked into my eyes as we repeatedly reached an intense and unforgettable release. Again and again as if she was reaching my soul, touching me beyond what anyone could see.

I had experienced no one in my life like I had Abbi; she said everything I was thinking. She saw in me what I found in her, a love and connection beyond our most profound dreams. There was something about us that made all the imperfections of my life become perfect. Every sad story in my life now lined with silver, becoming a stepping-stone on my path to Abbi.

When it was time to attend my class with Abbi, she approached me looking upset. I said, "Hey, how are you?" She replied "There was a substitute in my art class, and Jason groped me. The sub did nothing." Like a furnace igniting with a plethora of fuel I found myself overrun with feelings of frustration, but I held back, I didn't want to upset Abbi. As I grit my teeth I said under my breath, "It just had to be the school hero." She asked, "What am I supposed to do?" I responded, "I'll handle it." Abbi's arms crossed. Now looking at the floor, she said, "I told him to stop again, he seriously is just a jerk." I tried to be optimistic, I knew the more positive I was, the better she would deal so I looked up, smiled slightly, and said again "It's ok, I'll handle it." Just like I hoped, she smiled back, feeding off my encouraging tone and body movements. I said, "Let's go play yet another random game the gym sub comes up with." She nodded.

After gym class I walked alone to Ms. Robertson's office. Her door was open and she was alone, so I walked directly in. "Ms. Robertson" I said, she looked up with a slight smile, "Hello James." I continued, "I'm having a problem with Jason." She laughed and said "Jason? You mean the nationally recognized hero Jason? You mean the boy whose face was recently plastered on the wall in the cafeteria right next to his Uncle?" I replied, "He's been groping other girls and I'm pretty sure that's completely against school policy." Ms. Robertson sat up and placed her hands on the desk. "Girls?" she said. I paused for a moment, I didn't want to say it was Abbi because I knew she had issues with her in the past, but I didn't want to lie like this, so I responded, "Girl, one girl complained to me." Ms. Robertson responded, "What girl?" I quickly asked, "What does it matter?" She answered, "Because I don't believe anything Abbi says and, if it was Abbi, I won't feel any need to take action." I sighed deeply, completely fed up with Ms. Robertson's bias against

Abbi. "Well, I tried to handle this administratively and you failed to help" I said as I turned away to leave. Ms. Robertson sternly replied, "James, the girl is no good, she's damaged goods and…" I couldn't stand to hear that. I lost it and screamed, "How dare you! People like you are the real reason why this school got shot up in the first place! Demonizing everyone who disagrees with you, treating them like they are subhuman! I bet Seth had parents just like you, only showing kindness if they say and do exactly as you wish! But the moment they step outside your oppressive and small world, you shut them out and leave them for dead! Well guess what, we are all our own people! We all have burdens to carry and none of you should act like you would be any better when you haven't even tried to walk in the shoes of the people you ignorantly judge!" I slammed her door and stormed away completely unwilling to hear another negative word about the girl I loved.

After school had ended Abbi and I walked towards the busses hand in hand. In route, I scanned the area for Jason who usually hung out in front of school to sign autographs and take pictures with admirers who didn't actually know Jason personally. There he was, I spotted him. Just as I expected, bragging to other students right where I thought he would be. I told Abbi to get on the bus and save me a seat. She nodded but likely didn't know I was about to approach Jason.

Now quickly walking towards Jason I called out his name, he turned with an idiot smile painted across his face, "What's up second place?" I ignored his reference and said "I was told you groped a girl today. A girl that already asked you to leave alone." He replied, "Haven't you heard? I'm a stud around here. If I want to grab someone, it's gonna happen, and they'll like it too." I looked to his grinning jock friends behind him. I knew exactly what was going on in their minds and how they were aching for me to make a move so they could beat down yet another person who, in most situations, would have no chance.

Running Jason's comment through my head countless times in a matter of seconds, I confirmed my next course of action. "That's all I needed to hear." I turned away from him as he and his friends screamed "Wuss!" and other derogatory names to my back. Proceeding onto the bus, I asked Davis to walk Abbi home when they got to her stop. Abbi looked extremely concerned, but I, again, managed to control my posture and facial expressions so she would only see confidence. Wearing a warm and encouraging smile on my face, I handed her my bag, removing my skates from it as I set it down. I then kissed her on the forehead and said, "Don't worry, I'll be right behind you." She replied, "What why?" Just then Davis jumped up and said "Oh my god! You're going to beat their booties?"

I walked off the bus, locked my eyes on Jason & lurched forward in a full sprint throwing my skates down and pulling off my outer shirt as I approached a now turned away Jason. Only a couple feet away I quickly wrapped my twisted up outer shirt around his neck and used it guide his body backwards slamming him to the ground. I knew I had a small amount of time before he recovered so I rapidly and without hesitation kicked one of his 3 jock friends in the balls as hard as I could before he could react to assist Jason. As if it were a well-rehearsed sequence of moves I twisted to thrust my fist into another jock's throat. Now having successfully completed three moves on three unsuspecting targets, Jason's last friend in the group struck me as I expected, landing a punch on the side of my head. I reacted by spinning as I fell to the ground to deliver a sweeping kick the fourth and final target, knocking him on his back as well. This one was larger than the others so I made sure he would stay down by stomping on his balls before he could recover.

I turned back to the jock I had punched in the throat as if I was going to kick him as well, but he, unable to talk, signed that he was in no way interested in fighting. Now that I had successfully reduced the odds of their victory over me, I only had Jason to deal with. As Jason climbed back to his feet, he yelled "How is that fair! You fight like a crazy person!" Breathing heavily, I replied, "How is that fair? 4 jocks against one wuss like me? And what about you groping women who are too terrified to fight you off? How is that fair? How..." He full on tackled me before I could finish speaking. His tackle of Seth flashed in my mind as I flew backward with Jason's shoulder plunging just under my ribs. But I had no time to take a beating, the security guards were no doubt about to see what was going on and I couldn't finish what I started with them getting involved. We impacted the ground together; I tightened my abs just before impact in hopes I would be able to recover quickly. Jason grunted and jumped off me only to laugh forcefully as if showing off to everyone now gathered around us.

I wouldn't let Jason stand over me, I aggressively returned to my feet and with as much force as I could manage I launched at him with my right hand grabbing the side of Jason's head. Out of confusion he swung at me but I quickly jerked on his scalp and with it his line of sight darted away from the path of his fist. Simultaneously I shifted the position of my head so his hand would make contact with a cement pillar behind me. Distracted by the pain now engulfing his hand, I shifted my body to the left with all my strength while jabbing his throat repeatedly in the same direction. As he fell to the ground I leapt onto him using my knees and all of my body weight to pin his shoulder down. Like I had seen in school wrestling events I rapidly lined myself up to evenly distribute my weight on his strongest points so he could not fight back, I was right where I wanted to be. I smirked. My goal was about to become a reality. I was going to break his nose so that he could literally see in the mirror what happened to people who treated women like possessions.

He began to overpower me despite me strategically pinning him so I frantically pinched the tip of his nose with my strongest two fingers as he turned me over and with the other hand I punched the base of his nose repeatedly until I finally felt a pop. Jason quickly fell back to the ground screaming in agony. His reaction allowed me to stand up just in time for the security guards to reach us.

All the guards could now see was four jocks all grabbing different body parts in pain with me standing by breathing heavily, exhausted, but somehow slightly smiling. I was surprised I was able to pull off what I had intended with such accuracy.

Despite me being almost six feet tall I remained by far, the smallest in the group. Only the immediate witnesses could believe what they saw. I looked over to Abbi still on the bus to see both her and Davis staring out separate windows with their jaws completely dropped. I forced myself again to smile encouragingly and waved to Abbi as her bus began to pull away. It seemed like the fight lasted at least ten minutes, but I quickly became aware that it at most lasted only a couple.

Seconds later Principal Leeman came rushing out screaming, "What the hell just happened?" I looked at the jocks still struggling to recover and looked back at Principal Leeman without any significant indication that I was a part of the fight.

One of the security guards spoke. "I think the smaller one beat up the bigger ones" he said. Principal Leeman, still hysterical, screamed, "Where is the security camera footage?" Just then, a kid ran up to Principal Leeman and said, "You don't need no security footage, that dude beat all those jocks up!" The security guard added "We were told those weren't going to be actually functional until sometime next week." Principal Leeman looked at the guard like he just said the dumbest thing he had ever heard, he then looked back to the jocks, still incapacitated. "Anything to say? Anything?" he screamed. Jason spoke, now trying to stand up while grabbing his nose. "You guys don't say squat!" he said to his fallen friends. One of the jocks choked back "Couldn't... if... I wanted!" He continued to wheeze on the floor as Jason addressed the Principal, "Whatever just happened is *my* business! It happened to *me*, not you, or some tattle tale, so get over it

Leeman!" The Principal looked at Jason with disgust. "Your nose is bleeding and likely broken, you know that right?" he asked. Jason replied, "Well it's *my* nose, isn't it Leeman? It's *my* god damn nose, and if you want to cry to someone, make it your no doubt unsatisfied wife at home." There were no words to describe the look Principal Leeman gave Jason upon hearing what he said.

I stood in awe of how little Jason cared about having his face smashed up. Principal Leeman turned to me, frustration consumed his face and he clearly had no idea what to say. After only a few seconds he then looked back at Jason. "Under normal circumstances, your ass would be suspended for talking to me like that, today you get a warning Jason, shape up! That heroic stunt you pulled last year only goes so far. As for you, James, if you really did this, you're damn lucky the people you beat up are protecting you." Principal Leeman said continuing to scan all of us, he finished with "All of you, get the hell off my campus!" and walked angrily back into the school while screaming for the security guards to follow.

As Principal Leeman entered the building Ms. Robertson passed him to go home for the day. She was concerned by Principal Leeman's aggressive walking and immediately looked over at Jason, still holding his bleeding nose. When she saw me standing by the fallen jocks her face was overtaken by a look of horror. She clearly pieced together what had happened.

"Did you really have to bust up my nose like that?" Jason blurted at me upon the principal walking completely out of sight. I responded, "Yes, I absolutely had to. You don't grope women, especially not Abbi." He laughed, still holding his nose, "Oh! Abbi! Yeah, no, I was just joking around." I replied, "Well, we're not laughing. I'm sure you'd do worse to me if it was your girlfriend." His smile disappeared; in a serious tone he then said, "I would murder you." I replied, "Exactly."

A scream came from the background. "Beat his ass Jason!" one of his jock friends, still on the ground, yelled. Jason was clearly offended by their disrespect to him and screamed back "None of you touch him, if you have a problem, take it out on the field." Jason saw Ms. Robertson still staring. He hollered, "Hey Ms. Robertson, you want a piece of this or are you just zoned the hell out?" Looking offended, Ms. Robertson jolted back to life and continued walking off to her car.

Jason was acting like an ape to anyone who saw him bleeding, probably to hilariously attempt saving face. He turned back to me and said, "Listen, I'm sorry about your girlfriend and I'm also sorry to tell you, you didn't break my nose, I already did that myself too many times." Putting both hands in a prayer-like position on his face, he executed a swift motion to reveal his nose returned to its normal position. "You can't break what's already broken dude!" he said as he leaned over to pick up his jock friends.

I grabbed the skates I threw down earlier and began heading home. Abbi was waiting for me once I got there. She was so happy to see me, but also worried that I got in trouble. "You're not going to jail right?" she asked. I responded, "No. Apparently, when you beat some jocks up, they'll refuse to admit anything happened at all. Jason even chewed out the principal for asking." Abbi then asked "Well, I was about to take a bath to drown myself in worry but now that you're home, you can join me?" I replied with a smile, "Sure, of course."

As I went to sleep that night, I had conflicting emotions. I always hated chauvinistic men, but my first hand experiences with Jason proved that, just because someone acted like a disgusting pig in one area, didn't mean they had no honor at all.

The weeks passed by like a warm dream, but as summer approached, so did a yet to be known sorrow. Many of us like to think we're completely in control until one day, a painful and dark reality pays us all a visit, pulling the veil of lies from our eyes, leaving us shattered and lost.

CHAPTER 16

The days drifted by, we were getting to the end of the school year and today seemed like just another day. My mom was in town and didn't have a job in the area anymore so she let me take her car with the impression I was on my way to school. Abbi and I picked Davis up on the way, for the third day in a row, only this time we felt like exploring the surrounding area instead of going to school.

"Where do you want to go Davis?" Abbi asked. He replied, "I want to go to space!" I laughed and replied "Anywhere in the general area?" Davis said he wanted to go to the local park, but we wound up heading to a park we hadn't been to before which required we take the highway.

It was such a very sunny day; we drove with the windows down and laughed as we listened to the most absurd music. Davis did such a hilarious impression of every other lead singer we heard. We arrived at the unfamiliar park and tried the games they had installed there, one of them being a weird chain-Frisbee game. I imagine it was popular to have been installed in the ground with cement, I just hadn't heard of it.

Davis found a paper board sheet stapled to a tree; it was asking for everyone who saw it to sign it so the person who posted it could come back and take it to their local politicians to have their favorite drugs legalized. It kind of seemed like a careless way to do it as it was nowhere near as controlled or legitimate, as it would seem if they just went door to door. We entertained ourselves by writing down names like "Dick Wood and Harry Johnson" and whatever other childish thing we could think of. We definitely got a couple laughs out of the names we came up with.

As the day wore on we became hungry so we ate our sack lunches. Davis normally bought the school-issued lunch so we shared ours with him. Davis checked his phone and let us know school was about to be out; this meant my mom would be expecting the car.

As we drove down the road Davis kept sticking his head out the window like a dog, yapping and howling till he saw something that caused him to go completely silent. Abbi looked back and followed Davis' line of sight until she saw what he did. Slowing the car to see what was wrong, I realized tears were filling Abbi's eyes; she couldn't handle it and looked away to bury her head in my chest. What they had both seen was a man who had literally just jumped over a bridge that crossed over the freeway we were about to merge onto.

Without a second thought Davis stumbled desperately out of our still moving car towards what he perceived as a rapidly dying man. Not thinking about himself for a second, Davis had somehow made his way to the center of the four-lane freeway and tried to lift the man up so he could still have a chance at life.

My heart was pounding to a point where I felt like breathing was as difficult as lifting weights. I wanted to scream, reach out to save Davis and run away all at the same time. Cars screeched around Davis but he barely paid any attention to them. As we rushed closer to him, I heard him screaming to the man "It'll be ok Mr.! I'll…"

Davis couldn't even finish his sentence.

Not even the school shooting compared to seeing my friend obliterated on the highway as he tried to save a life that didn't even want to be saved.

A large van had just swerved to avoid Davis, but someone was tailgating behind the van and had no time to evade. Davis' entire body rose up and spun in the air, his head smacking against the pavement so hard you could hear the impact over the screeching tires. Abbi and I both screamed still trying to make our way towards him.

I was so overwhelmed seeing my friend, my only real friend, torn away from me in an instant. I didn't care if I was going to die too. I rushed out on the freeway grabbing and pulling him away so no other cars could strike his body.

Traffic came to a stop quickly after I pulled Davis off the road. Barely being able to see, my eyes blurred and filled with tears, I looked up at the hanging man Davis tried to save and, even through my distorted vision, I could see his neck was contorted in a strange way. I couldn't really understand it at the time. I was just sobbing; I hated myself for ever being in Davis' life because I knew if I never even met him he'd likely still be alive.

So many thoughts rushed into my mind as I held Davis, whose body remained completely limp, his neck further back behind his shoulders than I feel comfortable admitting.

He was going to change so many lives; he was going to share his happiness and humor with the world. I always thought he was bound for amazing things and I kept reminding myself of the reality that he would have had those things had I never been born. How could I not blame myself? I had never hated myself more than I did in that moment.

Abbi sat by me on the side of the road and we both sobbed long past the ambulance arriving. I overheard one of the ambulance workers saying the rope the man was hanging by had snapped his neck in the fall and was impacted by a passing truck before Davis even got to him. Had Davis successfully gotten him down, there wouldn't have been much chance of a life for the man anyway.

Abbi and I had to endure them telling us Davis had also died almost instantly when his head smacked against the road. They were telling us we were holding a boy who had passed long before they arrived. I couldn't stop crying no matter how hard I tried. One of my only friends was erased from my life, from the world itself, in an instant.

After they took Davis away I walked back to the car and laid in the back seat. Abbi tried to talk to me, but I couldn't say anything, I just cried softly to myself. She grabbed the keys out of my pocket and drove me to Davis' house. I envied her in a way, for not knowing Davis as long as I did, for not being able to hurt as much from the loss of him, as every day I was a around him, I missed him that much more now that he was gone. He had made a place for himself in my heart, and now all that was left was a sad shadow-consumed hole.

Abbi knew we had to make sure the hospital had called Davis' parents about what happened but as we arrived their cars were both still in their driveway. I couldn't walk so I just sat outside our car, leaning up against the back wheel as Abbi approached their front door. She rang the doorbell and Davis' mom answered. Davis' mom carried a smile for only a moment until she realized both Abbi and I were crying.

She asked where Davis was because she knew we picked him up earlier that day, and that's when we heard her phone start to ring in the background. Davis' mom had put everything together in a matter of seconds and began screaming with an intensity I never heard before. She ran over to me screaming as I remained hunched over, unable to move, "What did you do? What did you do? Where is Davis?" I just kept crying. I had no words.

She screamed "God damn it, don't you do this to me. He loved you and you do this to me?" She ran back into her house to answer the still ringing phone.

I was completely lost inside my own head. I had no escape; I only had the same images playing over and over again. I felt powerless and I couldn't stop saying "I hate you" to myself over and over in my own mind.

Had Abbi not been there, I would have never made it home that night. She was all I had left.

CHAPTER 17

Davis' funeral came too quickly, I couldn't imagine ever being ready to say goodbye. Sometimes I felt like it would be so much easier had it just been me, but then I would imagine Abbi being left alone and felt even more pain. I can't find solace in grand gesture of self-sacrifice, as it would mean hurting everyone else I love, and yet I'm struggling to accept the very reality that surrounds me.

I didn't want to say anything at his funeral; I could barely even manage to sit in the back with Abbi and my mom. I found myself looking down at the floor, drowning in my shame. Every other word spoken at the funeral only made me hate myself more. The cries of his family members, listening to them talk about the amazing person I already knew him to be, I just wanted to lose consciousness so I wouldn't have to endure my self-loathing any longer, but I had earned this torment, I had earned the disgrace I felt.

It was time for his mother to give a speech, I couldn't bear what I was about to hear but you can't deafen your ears as simply as you can close your eyes and even if I could, I was more than willing to hear her curse me. I deserved to know how much Davis's mom hated me for being in her son's life. It was only right that I would be reminded I was the reason Davis left this world far too soon.

She approached the podium that stood next to an enlarged picture of Davis surrounded by flowers. Davis' mom began to speak, "My son was the brightest light in my life. From the moment he was born, I could see happiness in his eyes. He always loved putting a positive spin on most everything around him, but despite his regular upbeat attitude, he..." she paused looking at the far wall behind us all. Collecting herself, she continued, "...we didn't spend as much time as we'd have liked if I'm going to be honest. I assumed, like many parents, that I would never see my child pass before I did." She paused again, looking down with her hands firmly clasping the podium. She said, "His father and I worked a lot, a ridiculous amount really. But we were able to create a comfortable life for Davis. We would have dinners every night together, and he would talk about everything that was going on at school only to return to his room whenever he was not eating with us or participating in some holiday."

"A lot of people will sugar coat what person they idealistically believed their kid to be, all I can really tell you is the truth, our son was literally perfect in every way. That is the complete and utter truth, no denying it whatsoever, he was an angel," she said as the room slightly brightened in its mood. She continued "When I was able to spend quality time with my son, he often spoke of his friend James. James, as some of you know, was there when Davis passed. He would always say how much he liked James and told me how handsome he thought he was. He said just being around James made him feel like he was cool, and part of something important." I sat there crying, listening to her not curse me as I suspected, but possibly even worse, make me hate myself more by revealing how much faith Davis had in me. The weight I felt on my shoulders increased knowing how much he was counting on me, and where was I?

I flashed back in my mind to the freeway, Abbi and I couldn't catch up with him; we tried, but were scared. Seeing that man hanging there, it was like something you would see on TV, a scene straight out of what you'd expect from a 3rd world country. We weren't ready for it, but Davis just ran without thinking about it, it's like he had no sense of self, he cared about a stranger more than himself while Abbi and I were crippled by the impossible choices we were faced with. It was only when Davis was hit that I was willing to put my life on the line and what did it matter? It was already too late. All because someone who gave up on the world and wanted to show them what he felt about it in one final act decided to foolishly do to others what others had done to him. The man who jumped from the bridge blamed the world and in that act, he caused a heart that was good, that pounded like a mighty drum, the heart of my friend Davis, to cease its song forever.

I looked up to see Davis' mom continuing to struggle, she managed to go on "I know James is angry at himself for what happened. I screamed at him when he showed up on my doorstep crying. Knowing Davis was with him, I held him responsible, but after talking to the emergency responders, after learning about exactly what happened, I realized James is actually the reason Davis is laying in this casket before us, instead of only ashes in an urn. He risked his life to pull Davis off the highway, that act of selflessness made me better understand why Davis looked up to James." Abbi squeezed my hand hearing what Davis' mom had to say. I was still shaking and grief stricken despite his mom trying to relieve me of the guilt I felt.

Abbi leaned over to me and said, "I love you James, I always will." Tears continued to run down my face, Davis' mom could see this too. Tears ran down her face almost in sync with mine. She stepped down the stairs by the podium and walked over to me. I stood up still looking down and consumed with shame. She wrapped her arms around me and I could hear other people gasping for air, I assume this moment was overwhelming for most everyone, but it was hard to think about much of anyone over the constant self-loathing screams saturating my mind.

My tears began to soak into Davis' mom's shoulder

so I lifted my head only to see her holding a brave but pain-filled smile as she looked upon me with tear-filled eyes. Davis' mom then returned up the stairs and I sat back down. I felt awful, but I could feel a small weight lifted, like I was just about to be crushed but was saved by a single embrace.

Davis' mom concluded her eulogy. "I don't want anyone to be angry over what happened to my son, but sadness is just our way of showing how much we cared for him. I think it's important that we all remember that there are pieces of my personality, your personality, every personality in this room, that are shared with countless other human beings on this planet. Your opinions, feelings and behaviors are very rarely exclusively experienced and expressed by any one individual. Accept it or not, none of us can really die, because every aspect of who we all are exists in our brothers, our sisters and even many complete strangers. Our playfulness, our capacity to love, everything that makes us who we are, is shared with countless human beings, some like us in many ways, others only sharing a few traits."

"I see Davis' smile in my husband," she said looking over to her husband who gave a small smile of encouragement as tears ran down his face. "I see his eyes in his grandmother. He also had many nerdy hobbies just like her as well" the room gave out a sad laugh as she continued, "We are all part of Davis, and

Davis is part of all of us. Live on knowing, so long as one of us survives, none of us can ever be completely gone." She concluded now looking down, tears falling from her eyes to the podium, "I love you Davis. When I miss you, I'll do my best to pay you a visit, through your father, through your grandmother and, if I'm alone, I'll do my best to see whatever part of you I can through myself." Her husband, Davis' father, softly greeted her as she walked off stage.

After the service Davis' mom approached Abbi and I and hugged us. She repeatedly reminded me that I was one of the best parts of Davis' life and that he would want me to be happy. She saw how much I was crying, how wrecked I looked; I couldn't really say anything to her, all I could do is hug her back and listen.

Davis' father also approached me, putting his hand on my shoulder and only said "You know…" He started crying and couldn't even finish saying what he wanted to say. I replied saying "I'm sorry" and he hugged me as if we were holding each other up. We were both so tired of crying, so weak, neither us having eaten much of anything in days.

My mom remained silent the entire funeral. She was supportive, but tried not to get involved because she didn't know how to process everything that had happened. Abbi and I sat in the back of the car holding hands the whole trip home. Just as she had many times before, she ran her fingers across the hairs on my hand, trying to comfort me.

When we arrived home, I went in my room with Abbi, she closed the door and we rested in bed the remainder of the day in silence. We were emotionally exhausted and sleep was a small break from the painful reality we had come to find ourselves living in.

CHAPTER 18

I couldn't miss any more days of school as Lakewood High had little tolerance for repeat absences. Had I not returned to school shortly after, they would invalidate the work I had already done that semester.

I had pretty much the same classes all year, Washington State history 1 and 2 covered my first and second semesters. My TA position was extended for the second semester. Meanwhile gym class had yet to see Mr. Mack return as far as I knew, but I hadn't been to school in a few days.

As I walked into school, it felt like nothing had changed, like no one knew Davis had even existed in the first place. Had they not lost over 40 people the year prior in the shooting, I would have been angered, but tragedy was becoming the theme of our school, and my own life. You could say we were all stronger because of it, but strength and numbness are two different things. When you can't feel anything because you've been beaten to a point where your senses stop functioning, you don't really have to be strong to endure it. To many people who remain in a state of numbness, every new blow is nearly indistinguishable from the strikes prior. Call it some twisted way to force us into surviving despite the conditions being unacceptable in most every way.

When my TA period began Ms. Robertson paid me a visit. She walked over to me grading papers and asked, "How have you liked working with Mr. Hanson?" I replied saying "I like it just fine." She looked over to Mr. Hanson and said "Would you like to tell him now?" Mr. Hanson smiled and walked to the front of his desk, he leaned against it, but his weight caused it to slide backwards. Quickly he stumbled to stand and blurted out "Yes! Absolutely! James, we were thinking of you taking on a special role next year." I looked at him, lacking any feeling or sign of enthusiasm, but he continued, "We wanted you to run for school president, and this whole TA business was just about figuring out if you're the right person for the position." I sat and stared at them as if they were playing a sick game with me, but they didn't know I had just a lost a friend, they only knew what I was willing to tell them, which was pretty much nothing.

"You really just messed with my schedule so I could run for a position that you didn't even know if I wanted?" I asked in a monotone voice. Ms. Robertson replied, "I know we've had our bumps, but judging by Mr. Hanson's positive feedback, you have the strength and sense of integrity we would look for in someone who was running for the school President." I replied, "So assaulting four jocks in front of the school, that was integrity?" Ms. Robertson's posture completely changed, she was clearly offended and replied, "You heard what that boy said to me! Obviously! He… and his friends! They…" I could see she knew she was about to say something that no guidance counselor could justify saying.

Mr. Hanson continued, "We believe in your decision making skills and, unlike other schools, the school President here has actual power. They have repeatedly in the past become a complete pain to deal with, we think you're different, and think you could actually do something good for the entire school instead of just causing a headache for the faculty." I replied, "There's no guarantee I'll be successful, you could have put all this faith in me for nothing." Ms. Robertson jumped and said loudly "We're not going to let the students have another election where they have only an idiot and moron to choose between. You will win because the people who are right for the job rarely want it. James, you're exactly the person who needs to do this." I looked down at my desk silently.

Mr. Hanson said, "You're a good kid, one of the best I think. I wouldn't say it if it wasn't true." Ms. Robertson proceeded to leave the room. I just felt surprised she was even willing to talk to me after I lectured her about her failures as a guidance counselor.

It felt like hours, but finally my TA class was over, and I headed over to gym class where I saw someone I didn't quite recognize standing in the middle of the gym. As I walked closer, I realized it was Mr. Mack, only with a massive scar on the side of his face that lead past his hairline.

"Mr. Mack!" I screamed. He turned to me and smiled, "Hey kiddo!" he said. With a smile on my face, I asked "I'm so glad you're back, how are you feeling?" Mr. Mack responded "Well, for a guy who got shot twice, not bad."

After a moment of thought I realized this was the first time I had genuinely smiled since Davis died. It was just nice to see the only teacher who really came close to bonding with me alive and well after his hospitalization.

Mr. Mack then reminded me I wasn't dressed for gym yet, so I ran off to the locker room. As I returned to the main gym I could see all the students surrounding Mr. Mack. In this moment, I felt a small piece of luck shine on me. It was now clear that despite my tardiness, I managed to come back on the first day Mr. Mack was back.

He had all of us play dodge ball, just like the first day I attended his class but, this time, Raymon was on my team and, just as before, our team was lucky enough to claim victory.

There was a decent amount of time left in class so Mr. Mack decided to tell us about his experiences in the hospital. His told us how many days he stayed there, how many surgeries he had to have and he also thanked us for the gifts and visits he received from many of the students.

As he talked, time flew by much faster than it ever did when we played games, likely because I had never heard about some of the things he talked about and found it really fascinating. Sitting in the hospital day after day post school shooting for as long as he did, Mr. Mack no doubt had played out the scenario he endured hundreds of times in his mind. I guess we were the right audience for him to let all his thoughts out to, I felt lucky.

As we left the gym together Abbi and I were holding hands as we always did. Walking outside to head to the building our classes were in I could see Ms. Robertson stomping towards us with a scowl on her face accompanied by two police officers.

I immediately thought of everything I had done wrong or felt guilty for and assumed I was finally being punished for the fight I had gotten in with the jocks, especially since I blatantly admitted what happened in my TA class earlier that day in the presence of Ms. Robertson. Contrary to my assumption by looking closer at Ms. Robertson's eyes I could now see she was focused on Abbi. She was staring at Abbi so intensely it was almost as if she hadn't even noticed I was even there.

A wave of fear overtook me. Nervously, I softly said "Abbi…" to alert her of the situation. Looking over at Abbi I could see she knew something I did not. Ms. Robertson loudly said, "Abbigale, I need you to come with us!"

Abbi looked at me with terror in her face. One of the officers grabbed her by the arm. I remained frozen. I was in shock and had no idea what to do. As they walked her away, she had her free hand on her face, as if she were guilt stricken by something. I was trapped in analytical state again. Having seen the guilty posture she had taken and the look in her eyes, I found myself consumed by the feeling that the person I loved most had betrayed me. How could I so quickly doubt her after all we had been through?

"The person I loved most…" I mumbled to myself aloud. I loved her more than anything or anyone. I didn't even care about whatever she had done, as it didn't make a difference. She was everything to me. Without a second thought, I chased after them, following them to Ms. Robertson's office.

The two officers took Abbi inside leaving Ms. Robertson outside the room. As I approached Ms. Robertson and her office she jumped in my face hysterically saying loudly "This is what I was talking about! This is why I warned you!" Her finger was shaking in my face but I ignored her clear emotional

imbalance and asked, "What exactly is going on?"
She replied, seeming somewhat relieved but strongly
condescending, "You've been dating her for how
long? And you don't know?" I replied, "No." She
answered "I can't tell you, but if she didn't pull you
in on this, well it just makes me happy that you're not
also an accomplice." "Accomplice to what?" I asked,
but Ms. Robertson took a step back, crossed her arms
and refused to say anything else.

Inside the office the police already had closed the
blinds, all I could hear was them talking in stern
muffled voices as Abbi responded softly in a
collected tone. I was happy that whatever was going
on, Abbi was handling it with a level head. I had
never known her to lose her temper or act irrationally,
but this event created fear and doubt that the person I
had fallen for may not have been who... no, no more
of this. I had to have faith in her. She didn't just
deserve my support, she relied on it, we both needed
to stand by each other through it all. Like two pillars
leaning against only the other; if one of us fell, we
would find ourselves both shattered to pieces on the
floor.

After about 30 minutes, one of the officers opened the
door to let her out. Abbi walked out, not knowing
how I would react and I immediately walked up to her
and hugged her. She whimpered with a sound of
relief. Ms. Robertson saw this and exploded into a

rage, screaming, "You're letting her go?" One of the cops replied, "There's no real proof she did anything." Ms. Robertson yelled, "She is responsible for everyone who died in the shooting! She told her boyfriend to do it! It was all in the letters you found in Seth's home! It was in her hand..." Ms. Robertson abruptly stopped speaking. Like an irresponsible child, she shouted something she could neither prove nor had the right to say. All she could do now is give up.

One of the officers replied, "Like I said, you're speculating, she didn't use the specific wording needed to... we literally just..." The officer paused and rolled his eyes, realizing none of his words were resonating with her. He continued "Never mind, you just go about your business and leave that girl alone." The two officers immediately began heading out as Ms. Robertson turned to us with an enraged look in her eyes.

I was still trying to cope with what I had just heard. Abbi turned to me looking worried that I was going to react as if I believed everything Ms. Robertson said, but I didn't. I couldn't take the side of a woman who was proving herself to be progressively losing her mind, and who also had a clear biased agenda over my beautiful, loving Abbi.

In a soft, slightly quivering voice Abbi said to me "I didn't say that, I promise." I replied, "Promises are for people who can't be trusted on their word alone, I'll always believe you Abbi." She grabbed me and hugged me as Ms. Robertson yelled "Oh you two are perfect for each other!" and I muttered in response with a slight smile "Perfectly imperfect." Abbi gave out a sad laugh, accompanied by her already falling tears in response. We never stopped reminding ourselves how wonderful it was to have each other and took so much pride in knowing we would always be there for one another.

I walked Abbi to her next class and headed over to mine immediately after. We were both late, but neither of our teachers seemed to care. The shooting changed how a lot of teachers treated us, and not just with tardiness. There we rules they'd regularly ignore that they never did before all for the sake of not upsetting us.

After school Abbi and I met on the bus, a sad vehicle that had become little more than a painful reminder we would never see Davis again. It amazed me how busses in general were completely ruined for me but I didn't have a choice in the matter and, even if I did, in a way the pain just brought me closer to him. I kept wondering when the heartache would end, maybe it never will.

Arriving home, Abbi closed the front door and said, "I need to talk to you." I walked over to my room, dropped my bag to the floor and sat on my bed.

"I told the police the truth," she said. I replied, "That you are completely innocent?" She responded "Not exactly James." I felt the familiar wave of panic overtake me, my heart giving me a horrible sinking feeling. My head lowered, I lost eye contact with her and I remained silent. She then said, "When I was dating Seth, I was really messed up, you know that." I maintained my silence, listening, hoping she wasn't going to say something that would rip me in half. "When I was depressed, and cutting, I told Seth in multiple letters that I wished everyone would just disappear. But that's..." Instantly, like a muscle response, I stood up, turning her remaining words into a silent panic and I walked into the bathroom, slamming the door behind me.

I began pulling off my clothes, alone in the bathroom and turned on the shower. Even the sound of the warm water shooting out of the shower head and smacking against the back of the tub couldn't disguise the sound of Abbi crying in the other room.

I got into the shower, collapsed on the floor, and lost myself in thought.

I was overwhelmed by the fact Abbi just admitted she told someone who wound up being a school shooter that she wished everyone would disappear. "She didn't tell him to kill anyone" I told myself, "She didn't say she actually wanted him to do anything," I

162

thought with my arms wrapped around my knees with my head resting on my arms. The water poured around the side of my face and into my eyes. I looked down to see I hadn't even remembered to remove my boxers. I felt like my life was just another sad tear drenched sob story and happiness was only the intermission.

I then asked myself "Who hasn't wished someone wasn't there? Who hasn't wished they were all alone when they feel like everyone around them doesn't understand them? That doesn't mean they want to see people to be shot… it doesn't mean they would genuinely want anyone to be subjected to that kind of suffering." I then reminded myself that we all make our own happiness. I could continue to view sorrow and emptiness as the main theme in my life, but this wasn't the fault of uncontrollable conditions, I had a choice. I was going to choose to stand up, turn off the water and return to catch the tears of the woman I loved.

Opening up the bathroom door still soaking, I could see Abbi across the hall looking up with tears still running down her face. She was scared; she didn't know why I had come back out. I approached her and lifted her up by the center of her back and back of her leg just as I had in the middle of her class some time ago. She cried giving me a sad scared look "I don't understand" as I pulled her close to me. I replied

"You didn't want anyone to die, you just wanted to be alone so no one could judge you or hurt you anymore. That's not uncommon, and you did nothing wrong." She let out a loud cry of relief and wrapped her arms around me.

I kissed her on the neck as I held her whole body. She gave out a tearful laugh saying, "You're all wet!" I smiled and laid her on the bed, kissing her as I removed her clothes. She kissed me passionately, smiling whenever our lips were seconds apart. She felt accepted and relieved.

I chose happiness.

CHAPTER 19

The next school day I walked hand in hand with into the school building and immediately saw most every set of eyes in the room turn to us. She stopped walking, realizing right away exactly why she was being looked at. What Ms. Robertson screamed in front of all the students in the hall had spread around the day prior like an infectious disease.

As we walked only a few yards past security, it became clear someone had planned to humiliate Abbi the moment they saw her. Our suspicion became a reality when someone ran up to her, throwing a can of black paint to cover her upper body, just falling short of her face. Abbi gasped as the paint collided with her clothes. They went to spit on her but by then my hand was already impacting the side of their neck, slamming them to the ground. Everyone began screaming "Oooohhhh!" a sound I had become sick of hearing every time a slightly stimulating event occurred in their no-doubt mundane daily lives.

The security guards were much faster to intervene this time due to us being immediately by the metal detectors. They rushed forward and escorted the three of us to the principal's office. I identified the small, skinny longhaired boy who threw the paint; it was Chris Jenkins, the class clown who mindlessly insulted the President of The United States during his visit to our school. Out of the three of us now being escorted, he was the only one security had to physically force to follow them to the office, but the guard seemed to drag his little body along with ease.

Abbi and I stood waiting in Principal Leeman's office as his I wiped the black paint off her neck and chest using paper towels Mr. Leeman's secretary gave us.

Abbi didn't seem too upset by what happened, but she was worried about the future. In a surprisingly strong voice, she said "This is only the beginning of it, people aren't going to be able to accept me like you. They never did and, with what they have now, they likely never will." I frowned slightly, wishing I could do something, but felt powerless. She went on to say "Rumors are like a poison, it doesn't matter what the truth is, what they want to believe, they will believe. When Ms. Robertson screamed what she did, she killed my future at this school." I wanted to argue, to give her some hope, but that would mean lying to her, the wounds from the shooting were too deep and they wanted someone within their reach to blame.

I turned to see Principal Leeman through the glass window on his office door. He was flailing his arms at his secretary just outside, likely upset that he had just started his day and a significant incident had already occurred.

He then looked over at me, still wiping Abbi off. He was so upset he was for a moment and at a loss of words. He just stood there staring at us through the door with his mouth completely open. As I turned back to Abbi, I could hear him scream "Oh my god! Why?" he was walking towards us looking at the ground, there was a trail of black paint leading to his office. Abbi and I couldn't have avoided getting it all over the place due to the security guards ordering us to walk in.

Opening the door angrily, Leeman screamed, "Where is the idiot who did this?" Abbi and I looked just outside the room towards Chris. Principal Leeman followed our line of sight to see the scrawny little kid shaking like a scared, lost animal in a chair just behind the reception desk. Leeman didn't even care that Chris was already terrified by his domineering presence. "You little idiot! You're going to be cleaning this carpets until they look better than new, you got me?" Leeman yelled. With a horrified yelp Chris screamed, "Yes sir I'm sorry!" Leeman now inches from Chris's face, mumbled something to Chris that no one else could hear. Whatever was said, Chris looked traumatized in response.

Principal Leeman stood fully upright, turned, and walked back into the room we were in, slamming the door behind him. "What the hell happened?" he screamed, I replied, "Recently Ms. Robertson gave everyone within hearing distance of her office the impression that Abbi was partly responsible for the people who were shot last year." He replied "She doesn't look like Seth to me!" I added, "Ms. Robertson was referring to notes Abbi had written." He belted out "I don't care about any of that! The only thing I'm concerned with is the fact that the person who, under their own free will, shot up my school is behind bars!" He continued, "Besides, if she had helped plot any of this she would be behind bars too! The cops already talked to me about it and cleared her name!"

We stood there silently, not having anything to say. He then asked "Anything else? You were just attacked or what?" Chris heard the principal through the door and screamed back "He assaulted me!" Principal Leeman looked toward the door, and then looked back at us "Explain." he said. I replied "After he threw the paint I…" Principal Leeman interrupted "I've heard enough, get out of here." I begin to leave as Abbi began to speak to Leeman, "Principal Leeman, I don't know if…" He cut her off saying "I'll take care of everything, got it?" Abbi nodded, hoping he knew what she was going to say.

As we walked out, I could see Chris glaring at us, only to hear a scream "Get in here, right now!" from Principal Leeman. Chris flipped like a light switch from angry glare to wide-eyed terror.

We approached Abbi's class worried that she would face more repercussions for what Ms. Robertson had said in the hall. Just then a voice came over the intercom, it was Principal Leeman, "It has come to my attention that a lot of you believe a student in our school, outside Seth Wilson, was in-part responsible for the shooting that took place last year." He then began yelling, "That is not at all relevant or true! And if I see any of you picking on any student, blaming them for the actions of the boy we all know is alone 100% responsible and is now in prison, I will not hesitate to suspend you and, for a lot of you, a suspension means repeating this semester." As he cleared his throat, Abbi looked at me with relief, "Again, whatever you have been told, by any students or staff about anyone being even remotely responsible for the shooting, outside of Seth, is a blatant lie and should be reported to me so I may deal with those dishonest individuals directly. Speaking of which, Ms. Robertson, can you please report to my office? That is all." The microphone squelched off and the entire building went silent.

Abbi looked at me amazed that the principal had shown complete intolerance for what had or would happen to Abbi as a result of Ms. Robertson's unprofessionalism. "Uh… Abbi, about the paint on your…" I began to say but Abbi interrupted "Oh stop, I'll set a fashion trend or something I'm sure". Abbi hugged me and said "See you at gym class hubby!" Thrown completely off, I breathlessly said "Hubby?"

She laughed and walked in her class closing her door behind her.

I returned to my class and Mr. Hanson was, to no surprise, sweating from his forehead while reciting more boring facts about Washington State. I sat down and immediately began trying to figure out from his body movements if he was worried about Ms. Robertson. I knew those two had a pretty close relationship as far as school staff goes but I figured I'd find out after class about how he felt anyway so I didn't look too far into it.

Mr. Hanson had us all give reports on a specific part of Washington that we had visited in our lives that we liked. I had nothing prepared so I just went off the top of my head. Only a few words into telling the class about where I had been and Mr. Hanson screamed "A+!" The class laughed and I finished telling my story with just a little boost of optimism thanks to his outburst.

As I completed TA work for Mr. Hanson, he brought up Ms. Robertson just as I expected. "Do you know what that whole business was with Ms. Robertson?" he asked. I replied, "It's really complicated." He then added, "I hope they fire her." I was speechless; I thought he got along with her just fine. He could see my disbelief so he explained, "Ms. Robertson is one of the most manipulative, judgmental and possibly insane women I've ever met. I'm only telling you this because I've never heard Principal Leeman that angry before, and I'm pretty sure that means she's getting canned." I replied "I don't know, like I said, it's complicated." He asked "Why are you so hesitant to speak your mind?" I replied, "Because it's not about just Ms. Robertson, there's a lot more to it." He then smiled and tilted his head back, stretching out his double chin to briefly become one chin, "Oh, it's about your girlfriend too." he said. I smiled, and replied, "Like I said…" he jumped forward and interrupted "Get back to work you!" but said it with a smile so I knew he was just trying to ease the tension.

As gym class came around, Abbi was all cleaned up and looking like her normal self. She was happy to see me, still giggling about calling me "hubby" earlier. I was so psyched to see her and feeling happy despite all that was going on.

Mr. Mack came out and told us "The game of the day is basketball! And if you don't want to play that, you must sit on the side lines and cheer every time someone scores a basket!" We all laughed as I ran to join in on a game. Abbi stood by the side with some other students and cheered for us just like Mr. Mack asked.

I think we were all just looking to have fun; even Raymon was being a good sport. I knew if it were earlier that year, he would have fouled me and other students only to act like he was the victim if anyone called him on it. Everything we all went through just seemed to bring us closer together, it was like a wall casting a massive shadow, but all any of us could look at was the tiny glint of light shining through the cracks.

I'd never heard Abbi cheer like this before so seeing her light up every time I scored a basket gave me a familiar goofy grin and only motivated me to do better. As I played I kept thinking about how everything could have gone to hell had I given in earlier on, but I was reminded that it wasn't only Abbi and I who found ourselves laughing our way through everything, but most of the students in our school. It was as if all of the tears shed in our school cleansed us of our differences, bonding us in a way most other schools would never know.

Abbi and I met at the bus and rode home quietly in our usual seat towards the back. She rested in my arms as if she didn't have a single worry and, in that moment, I found peace as well.

As Abbi closed her eyes, I stared off towards Davis' old seat. I imagined him cracking jokes and laughing; he could almost always offer endless entertainment. Just then, I felt Abbi's hand touch my face. "James" she said in a gentle tone, "Are you ok?" I just realized she had her hand on me to wipe a tear away. I didn't even know it had fallen, "I'm fine" I said. I looked at her, squeezed her gently, and smiled "I'm fine."

CHAPTER 20

Quite a few days had passed since Abbi was doused with black paint. We woke in each other's arms to the sound of my alarm clock. I wondered why I kept it all this time; it was such a random piece of crap. Sometimes it would go off in the middle of the day, other times it would go off at the right time. Abbi and I would always laugh because it had a delightfully annoying little chirp to it. Not so annoying you passionately hate it, but just enough to make you want to shut it off as soon as humanly possible.

We normally woke up based on our internal clocks, which worked because we rarely went to bed at an excessively late hour. Fortunately today, my little piece of junk alarm gave us some extra time before the bus arrived. Seeing we didn't have to leave right away Abbi kissed me good morning and told me she was going to make some eggs.

While she cooked I cleaned up our room. For some reason her talent for finding the strangest places to discard her clothes made me laugh inexplicably. Her now dried shirt covered in paint was crumpled on the floor. Just looking at it gave me the strange inclination to fold it into a square and pin it to the wall using thumbtacks.

When I was done Abbi walked in with two plates in her hands and saw the shirt on display. She said

"Well, that looks kind of cool." I replied, "I feel like, at this point, most bad things that happen won't really hurt us unless we let them." She set down the plates and hugged me; I said, "You turn bad things into beauty Abbi." I pointed at the shirt, "It's like the moment that paint hit you, it became perfect." She replied sarcastically reaching her arms out "You've gone too deep James, where'd you go?" I laughed hysterically, hugging her as she laughed as well. "Thank you James," she said. I kissed her on the forehead and softly continued laughing.

We waited that morning at the bus stop for about 40 minutes before we gave up and returned to our room. Abbi tried calling into school, but no one answered so we turned on the TV hoping to see if the local news said anything.

Before we could even flip to the news station, we quickly found most every local station was showing the same thing. At first, we thought it was just a random fire when Abbi raised her hand to her face in shock and said "James, that's our school."

I looked at her in shock and then back at the TV to read the scrolling news feed at the bottom of the screen. It read "Unknown arsonist suspected of starting fire that claimed most of Lakewood High." Abbi and I were now both sitting staring at the TV. The feed cut to a ground reporter who had approached a very upset Principal Leeman. As the reporter asked him questions, he kept apologizing to them, following it by "I can't comment at this time." He ended the conversation saying he had to deal with the situation and spun around looking at the school in disbelief, likely having no idea what his role now was, or how to even proceed forward after witnessing his job literally going down in flames right before his eyes.

Abbi and I spent the days after keeping each other busy at home, all the while expecting a call from a member of the school administration to explain what had happened.

We watched the news every day to learn updates on the story. It didn't take the fire department long to figure out how the fire had started. They confirmed it was in fact a result of arson. After talking to the staff in depth, the police were pointed towards the recently fired Ms. Robertson.

Just as we learned about her being suspected, our phone rang. I answered and the voice on the other end was of someone representing the school district. They confirmed my name and that I attended Lakewood High, following their confirmation with a briefing. "As you are well aware by now, the school suffered a major fire and is irreparable at this point. All of your class information and grades were stored in an online database so none of your information has been lost. Regardless, to make things easier for the staff and the students, we have decided to credit everyone as if they had already finished up the year." I asked for clarification and they confirmed that we would be attending an entirely new school the next year. To my relief they also said we would be proceeding to the senior class with our credits intact. I thanked them and disconnected.

Abbi and I were both happy to know the only thing the fire harmed was the physical school itself. In reality, not even a janitor was harmed as, by the time the fire had started, he had finished his work and gone home for the night. The administration really stepped up and made sure none of the teachers suffered financially and the students didn't lose any time.

Days later, Abbi and I decided to visit the site of our burned down school. The front was completely cordoned off so we approached Lakewood High from the back. As we got closer we could see the gymnasium building remained completely intact due to it being detached from the rest of the school. As a result, amazingly enough, the jocks were still allowed to use the facility itself and the unscathed field nearby for practice. Although I imagine they were doing it just to stay in shape for the next year.

The back area was pretty open so we were able to walk right up to a point only a few yards away from the fire damaged area. As we looked on, someone came up behind us, saying "Hey chump!" I turned to see it was Jason in his sports gear, he had seen us walking in from the field he was actively practicing football in. "Did you see the news?" he asked. I replied, "Last I heard they were looking for the arsonist." He laughed and said "Nope! They found her." Abbi and I looked at each other and then back at him, waiting for him to tell us who it was. Jason threw his arms out and screamed "It was crazy Ms. Robertson dude! She's all locked up now!" Abbi and I didn't know how to react, "You're sure? Last I heard it was speculation." I asked and he responded "Yeah! She didn't have to admit to it, but she still did. She said the school was like, rotten to the core and talked about how the renovations were just a lie covering up a bigger lie or something like that." There was a silence as the information soaked in, but Abbi broke right through it by busting out laughing throwing her hands to her knees hunching forward beside me. I smiled and Jason gave her a slightly bewildered look. Abbi's laugh was rich with satisfaction; it was an obvious victory for her after all the grief Ms. Robertson consistently gave her.

"Anyway! So, see you at the new school huh?" Jason asked. I replied, "Yeah, I guess." Jason then turned and ran back off to the field. Abbi's laughter was trailing off now as she returned fully upright. "You ok Abbi?" I asked, she replied with a smile, "Yup hubby, I'm just fine."

She and I turned around to continue looking at the burnt school. Suddenly I realized something; a small smirk crossed my lips…

"Well, I guess this means I won't be running for President."

39796248R00102

Made in the USA
San Bernardino, CA
03 October 2016